T0037747

THE RAZ/SHUMAKER PRAIRIE SCHOONER BOOK PRIZE IN FICTION

EDITOR KWAME DAWES

BOUNDLESS DEEP, AND OTHER STORIES

Gen Del Raye

UNIVERSITY OF NEBRASKA PRESS

LINCOLN

The University of Nebraska Press
is part of a land-grant institution
with campuses and programs
on the past, present, and future
homelands of the Pawnee, Ponca,
Otoe-Missouria, Omaha, Dakota,
Lakota, Kaw, Cheyenne, and
Arapaho Peoples, as well as those
of the relocated Ho-Chunk, Sac
and Fox, and Iowa Peoples.

∞

Library of Congress
Control Number: 2023007283

Set in Janson by Mikala R. Kolander.
Designed by N. Putens.

Contents

1

2

Author's Note

This book contains discussions of suicide. If you are in a crisis or feel that you are at risk, you can dial 988 in the United States to reach the 988 Suicide & Crisis Lifeline. Numbers for other crisis centers around the world can be found by going to www.findahelpline.com. Some stories also deal with themes of sexual assault and war. Please read with care.

BOUNDLESS DEEP, AND OTHER STORIES

1

We are brave children of braver
parents, born into a web of nouns.

—Yiyun Li, *Where Reasons End*

赤い靴はいてた女の子
異人さんにつれられて行っちゃった
横浜の埠頭から汽船に乗って
異人さんにつれられて行っちゃった
今では青い目になっちゃって
異人さんのお国にいるんだろう

The girl who wore red shoes
was taken away by outsiders
On a steamboat from the pier in Yokohama
she was taken away by outsiders
Now she must have blue eyes
in the land of outsiders

—Noguchi Ujō, from 赤い靴
(Red Shoes), a popular children's song

Hideto, in Motion and at Rest

Most of the time when I think of Hideto, I am waiting for a train. It doesn't matter where. I could be in Minneapolis, or San Leandro, or back home in Kyoto. There's something about the noise of train stations. How they sound vast and empty, like a cathedral, even when they're nothing but a raised curb on one side of the tracks. I lean forward, close my eyes, and wait. A body settles down beside me, and for as long as I hold my eyes closed, it's Hideto, back from the dead, matching his breaths to mine.

It must be because of something I heard from his father. Years ago, when I was back home for the winter, I visited Hideto's father in Akashi with a stew from my mother and a loaf of bread from my father. My father had sliced up the bread and packed it into half a dozen freezer bags. My mother had poured the stew into four Tupperwares. On the way over, for the whole three-hour journey, I felt the warm stew against my shins under the seat of the train. A rainy day, and the train windows were grimed with fog. When I reached the station Hideto's father met me by the turnstiles with a shopping bag and an umbrella under his arm, looking as though he were the one arriving from somewhere else. If you didn't know him, you would have thought he was lost.

He didn't look sad, exactly, but restrained. I think he had learned by then that there was no point in saying the things he most wanted to say except to certain people and at certain times.

Your parents know I can cook, right? he said when he saw what I had brought, and then laughed.

I didn't know him very well. His son, Hideto, and I had been friends in high school, but we both lived far away from school in opposite directions, and we never visited each other's houses. Also, it was less that I was friends with Hideto so much as that we were comfortable around each other. He was the captain of my soccer team and I thought the world of him. He was quiet and dependable in everything. We could sit next to each other on the spiky dead grass next to the field after practice with our shin guards half pulled off, feeling the pain ease into our feet as we leaned back on our hands, looking at nothing, and not feel the need to speak.

I met his father at graduation and sometimes at away games, where he showed up near the end of matches to drive Hideto home. I never saw his mother until the funeral. They had gotten divorced when Hideto was in middle school. She had moved back to Colombia not long after. Hideto would visit her once or twice a year, in winter or summer.

We're worried about Tetsuo, my parents had said. This was in 2009, when Hideto had been dead for three years. I was home from grad school, for two weeks in December before I had to go back. My parents were one of a group of parents from my high school who took it upon themselves to check in on Hideto's father immediately after the funeral, to make sure, in those first weeks, that he was fed. Even now, from time to time, they would visit him to drop off pies or pickled vegetables. He lived not too far from the new airport that had opened up in Kobe, and they would drive the extra twenty minutes or so on their way to budget vacations in Chiba or Okinawa. They said Hideto's father seemed split into halves: on some visits he would be happier than anyone, on others he barely spoke.

I thought it was probably a matter of grief. How there was now a part of him that was consumed in the loss of his son, and another, smaller part of him, that was capable of moving on.

At his house he made me tea and apologized that he didn't have any dessert or snacks to serve. He really seemed to have nothing to eat. Eventually he warmed up the stew on the stove and poured it into two bowls. We ate my parents' offering at his dinner table, facing each other on two plastic stools.

He talked about his espresso maker. This was a gleaming copper machine he'd bought last month. When it came up to temperature, it sang him a section of a song that turned out, when he finally tracked it down on the internet, to be an air composed by Louis XIII. He'd named the machine Kinako, like a kitten. He was one of those メカラブ族 (a mecha lover), meaning he obsessed over appliances the way some childless couples obsess over pets. This had always been a bad habit of his, even when he was a college student comparison-shopping washing machines he couldn't afford. He said he tended to get lost in his head, he called this 自家発電 (in-house power generation), and then he got up to use the bathroom, he called this ワシントンクラブ (the Washington Club) because of the initials WC, and when he came back I thought he had maybe been crying.

I was thinking of a time I met him at the station, he said, and I knew, of course, that he was talking about Hideto.

Hideto had dropped out of college a few years before he died. The college had been abroad, in Florida, and when he dropped out in his third year, he ended up living with his father in Akashi. It took him a while to find a job at a café in Sannomiya, and after that he started looking to move out. It shouldn't have been too difficult, he was fine with a cheap rental, and he had his father to cosign the lease, but it took some time. Hideto was different when he came back from Florida, unsure of himself, often late to appointments, full of nervous energy when he called me on Skype. He'd had a rough time in college, though not in any dramatic way, at least as I understood it; just in a quiet, lonely way that ground him down and left him in the fall semester of his third year on academic probation, failing all his classes. He'd never lived abroad before. He didn't have much of a problem with language—our high school was an international school—and there was me, in California, who was doing okay. This made it easier to blame him for failing.

Tough love. This is what his father thought was needed. After the divorce, he'd maybe treated his son too indulgently. He wasn't much good at getting angry, but he tried: he set a hard deadline for the move-out, charged rent for use of the house, told Hideto it was time to shape up.

The day he didn't come home on time, Hideto had toured an apartment in town with a realtor. He should have been done by three. At six, Hideto's father tried calling him, but no one picked up. At six-thirty, in the gathering dark, Hideto's father put on his coat and headed outside. It was early March, a clear day, just cold enough to see his breath. Something told him to head down to the station. A gut feeling, maybe, or a parent's aimless worry. He walked down the hill, through the old shopping center, across the bridge. He walked into the station building and used his monthly pass to get through the turnstile. In the end, he was a softy every time.

Hideto, he said. The boy was sitting on a bench on the train station platform. He had a jacket, but had taken it off, had folded it neatly at his side. Even from a distance, he looked cold. His shoulders were chicken bones. You could see them through layers of clothing, the way they stuck out, how sometimes Hideto's father would hold his son by the shoulders and they were thin and cold as two metal bars.

How long have you been here? Hideto's father said.

I don't know, Hideto said.

Is there something wrong? Hideto's father said.

I'm just tired, Hideto said.

Come home, Hideto's father said. You can rest up at home.

And still, for a minute, for two whole minutes, the boy wouldn't move.

After he died, Hideto's father said, I was angry at him for a long time for not opening up to me. He never seemed to want me to help him. When he died, I thought, If only I had known, there was so much I could have done. I know it wasn't simple, that it wasn't just because of one or two things, but still, I think there must have been something, maybe a few things, where if they got better, it would have made a difference, because he would have seen that things could change. But then, the other day I was thinking some more about it, and I decided something. Because all of you (and here Hideto's father looked at me squarely across the table, his left hand holding his right wrist, as though to comfort it), all of you kids, his old classmates, are keeping secrets, aren't you?

When I met Hideto's mother at the funeral, I recognized her voice. This was the first time I had met her. She was greeting an old neighbor, standing a little distance away from Hideto's other relatives, in a plain black dress, so that she could have been a friend or an old teacher waiting to speak to the family. I had never heard her before, but still, I knew.

It was Hideto's goofing-off voice. Or it wasn't that voice exactly, but what that voice was an echo of. Like a cover of a song in another language. I heard his mother speak and what I was listening to was Hideto after a long day, lounging on the train, the sun coming in low through the windows or filling an awkward silence between strangers, the easy joke outside a convenience store or waiting in line, a quick laugh about nothing.

We all did it. All of us kids with one parent who was from another country and one parent who was not. We wouldn't have dreamed of making fun of our mothers or fathers, but all the same, we never used those voices where we thought they could hear it.

We kept all kinds of secrets. Many of them were small secrets, and a few were big secrets we intended to take to the grave. We kept them both from our parents who were immigrants and from those who were not. We were often ashamed of them, our parents. That was one secret. We wanted to protect them. That was another. And we believed we were becoming them, which scared us, and this was a secret we kept even from ourselves.

Yes, Hideto's mother was saying to the neighbor at the funeral. Yes, he *was* an extraordinary child. But she was using that goofy voice, Hideto's voice, where the stresses were all wrong and the l's were r's.

It was like meeting an old, forgotten, and embarrassing friend. I remembered the context in which I had been fond of that voice, in which I had found it funny, and then I remembered the person I had been when that was true.

Though I'd never met Hideto's mother, I knew some things about her. She spoke in an accent. The pitch of her voice often dipped at the end of a sentence. She held one hand aloft in front of her chest when she spoke about subjects she was passionate about. She preferred not to use chopsticks. She couldn't read menus, though she was always up for a challenge, and she would try.

I can imagine Hideto, that day at the station, knowing he was becoming her. I can imagine the exhaustion of this. The bone-tiredness. This thing we tried very hard not to know. The private work we had always done of listing the various reasons that would make a difference. Our place of birth, our citizenship, our perfect pronunciation. Our careful schooling, our good teachers, our beautiful or terrible or forgettable faces. Our good nature, our sense of home, our youth, ourselves. How we tried to believe we would never not belong to this country or another in the eyes of friends and strangers in the way that our mothers or our fathers did not belong.

I can imagine how exhaustion pins him down. How it pulls him into his body so that he can't move. I can imagine that it's his future, how clearly he can see it, how it stretches out endlessly in front of him, that does this.

That day, at the apartment viewing, his future confronted him. The property manager, a small woman who could have been his grandmother, had turned him away. This was outside the front door of a faded pink building in the outskirts of the city that had bars on all the first-floor windows. There were factors that led up to it. The property manager had expected, based on Hideto's full name, to see someone with a native-looking face. The realtor, who had been recommended by a colleague of his father, had probably never shown rooms for clients who tend to get mistaken for foreigners and didn't know that it was better to explain things in advance and be rejected over the phone than to make the whole trip and be rejected in person. And there must have been luck as well, the age of the property manager, the inconvenience of the location, how maybe this was the first time the property manager had had to decide what to do in this situation. Look, she said. She was surprised into anger. You're not a Tsuneishi Hideto, she said, and you can't stay here. And then she turned to the realtor, holding out her hands. Help me, she said. Can you explain this in his language?

I'm a citizen, Hideto said, I'm half Japanese. But that didn't help. There were various reasons. How would the neighbors feel. How would she trust him to know about trash days and earthquake preparedness. What if he went back to "his country," and if he didn't pay rent.

It must have been, not the fact of the turning away, but the memories that rose up afterward, on his way home, that hurt him most. The things he said for years without hearing himself say them. There would have been many examples, but one might have come to mind. This was in a bank. There had been some sort of question about his citizenship in relation to the type of account he wanted to open. He asked if he could return with his passport on another day and they told him he should. When he did, a few days later, the same smiling man was sitting at the desk. He gave Hideto a new account. He told him the new card and pin would be arriving in the mail. And at the end, as though it were nothing, he handed back the passport and said, The next time you visit us, you should bring this from the start.

Okay, Hideto said, as though it were nothing.

His mother would have understood. But he couldn't tell her. He would have sooner died than let her think he was exhausted by the consequences of having been born to her.

His father would have understood. But he couldn't tell him. He would have sooner died than let him think he was exhausted by the consequences of having been born to the family he chose to create.

Sometimes, on Skype, Hideto told me. But what could I do?

What I'm describing is not the trigger. It's not the reason, or the worst of it. Between the day at the station and the end there were years of counseling, attempts, hospitalizations, new beginnings, recoveries. He called me sometimes for days in a row and sometimes, for years, he hardly called at all. He was all of the things during these years that he was when I knew him best. He was dependable, he was stoic, he was giddy, he was wise, he was pensive, he was breakable. I can imagine him in any way, but usually, in quiet moments, at a train station, I imagine him on the bench beside me.

I do this, I think, exactly because it isn't the worst of it. Because it's the best possible moment of it. Because it's him resting. In my mind, when I imagine this, he is alive again, and he is resting. He has been resting for years. He needs all the rest he can get, and in the life I imagine for him, he is going to get it. Day after day, for years and years—he sees no one, does nothing but rest. For a few moments, as he sits beside me, we rest together. We breathe together. And at the end of it, when we open our eyes, I feel the hand on my shoulder of a lost-looking figure, a worried mother or father, helpless, bending over us, who cares.

Hideto Worn Down in Gainesville, 2001

It isn't that anything specifically happens to him in college. He doesn't understand the people around him, even when he understands the words they are saying, even in those times when he understands the things they are referencing and he loses track of himself. He finds he rarely knows what he is about to say until after he says it. He finds himself listening to his own voice and wondering if he is serious or joking. He finds himself doubting whether he likes the things he thought he liked, whether he even did the things he thinks he remembers. Getting out of bed is difficult, or if not difficult, not something he often tries to do. And then, in October, there is an incident where a classmate with a collie mix apologizes to him for the behavior of his dog. The dog doesn't seem to be doing anything odd. It walks under the long office tables they are sitting at in a seminar and nuzzles his leg. He scratches it behind its ears. It tilts its head up at him with an expression of lazy pleasure, lets out a faint whine, and trots back to its owner.

You have to understand, the classmate says. Nigel doesn't like Asians. He's a rescue from a restaurant. And then he goes on at great length about the restaurant, how close Nigel had been to becoming someone's dinner. There is talk of pots and knives and procedures Hideto knows nothing about. Passers-by are horrified on his behalf, but Hideto finds he doesn't care much either way about what is being said. He only has a sudden urge to bend down and hug the dog, or else to lift it to his chest and run out of the building. Out of a whole classroom, in the middle of a crowd, this dog has seen him. Even if it hates him, or is afraid of him, it knows where he is from. This buoys him for days, the thought that something about him is concrete, is visible even to animals. That Friday, for the first time in months, he goes to both lunch and dinner on the same day. In his dorm room he opens up Skype and calls an old friend from high school. They talk for hours, late into the night. He thinks, just before sleep, I could go home. I could.

And then there are other things, that make him angry. A boy in line at the dining hall who learns where he is from and explains, to his friends behind him, about foreigners traveling through Asia for sex. How he calls it "yellow fever." How he uses the word "trapped." Trapped by children. How he thinks of his parents. How they tried to stay.

He is failing all his classes. Emails and letters have gone to his father in Akashi. His mother doesn't know.

My Mother Takes Me to a Public Bath, 1986

Because it is summer. Because it is late. Because my father has been gone for weeks now, and will be gone for weeks more still, and it is a late summer evening, that time of dusk when the sky seems to burn brighter than it has all day, the cicadas winding down the springs on their music box, the sun shining from behind stained glass above the dark silver of the trees. I am young, still young enough to be led away by the hand from the frayed, navy curtain that says Men to the one the exact color of clay in the creases of my palms. Three coins to the woman at the window in exchange for white towels the size of dinner plates, and a slotted wooden locker key the size and shape of a stack of my father's old Gakken workbooks rotting under the cracked plastic of the potted basil in the kitchen at home. The woman at the window leans over her counter until I can see her missing teeth beneath the prune of her lips, and she winks at me and calls me cute, and I, a child who expects nothing less, squeeze my mother's fingers, twist from the anchor of her hand like a chime.

On to the creaking wooden platform of the changing room, then through the sliding glass doors, frosted by steam, into the blue-tiled world of the bath. I am freed here from my mother's grasp while she takes a seat by a row of faucets to rinse off her tired and neglected body and I carry out an inspection of every tub—their cloudy depths, their peeling mirrors, the centipede seams of the silver duct tape sealing their edges against the walls. I stand in front of the ice bath, which I hate, and then the grass-colored scented bath, which I am not yet ready to chance. The simple, main bath, which is a wind-blown lagoon under the blue arms of a painted Mount Fuji, is beautiful and absurd to my eyes, but it is nearly full, so I turn to the last tub, from which a lone woman, soaking in water up to her neck, raises a pink hand and beckons me. Her fingers still pearly with water are thin and flawless, with eggshell knuckles and milk-glass nails, and I, a child who confuses kindness with beauty, will remember those perfect fingers in ten year's time when I overhear my father, just back from a trip to Kyushu, tell my mother about how poor Yukari's apartment was found empty, how she must have taken her things and disappeared to god knows where in the middle of the night.

You're Yūko's boy, aren't you? she says to me now, narrowing her searchlight eyes, her one raised hand fluttering aimlessly from her cheek, to her neck, to the water. You ever try an electric bath? she wants to know.

The tub is small and deep and perfectly square, and the water is clear enough that I can see the woman's rose-colored thighs stretching under the pebbled surface like railroad ties bleached by the sun. There is nothing odd about this tub, nothing out of place, nothing that makes it seem like anything more than a simple bath of warm water except a sign carved in white plastic grayed by time and steam.

I shake my head. I am too young to read more than a few simple words.

Well, come on in then, she says, and she turns her legs to the side to make room, but I stand on the wide, flat rim, unsure.

You afraid? she says, and smiles. She reaches her perfect fingers out for mine, and I watch her shoulders lift out of the water, and then the cushioned branches of her collarbones and the closed eyelids of the folds beneath her armpits pointing inward toward her chest. And I am watching these things rise toward me until I am suddenly in the water, my world turning gray, and there are invisible beetles with hard, delicate mandibles pricking at my elbows, at the webbing between my fingers, jogging down the knuckles of my spine. It is warm and dark in this swirling water where the beetles carry off my body piece by piece until there is nothing of me left, my five-year-old body unraveling, turned to soup, drifting away, and it is a shock how, after the initial surprise, it seems like the gentlest of dreams, this untying of my skin, this peeling away of the petals of my bones.

Later, when I tell her this, she spins me in the water until I am facing away from her. In the clouded distance I glimpse my mother twisting in her seat, scanning the room, but the woman behind me passes her hand over my eyes and I am alone again with her whispers in my ear.

Like a sugar cube, she says. Easy. *Poof.*

Yukari Kneeling in My Mother's Garden, 1994

We had been sent out of the house to collect turnips. I was thirteen and Yukari was ageless, I thought then, as anyone above twenty-five seemed ageless to me, though now I think she must have been in her late thirties, maybe thirty-eight or nine, with a daughter my age and a husband she was grieving while he was still alive. She had come up to the house for lunch, a sort of party, though there were no other guests. She arrived in a new car, a cheerful green hatchback; a new yellow blouse, with diamond-shaped cutouts on the shoulders and down the arms; and a leather shoulder bag, which she tossed over a chair when my mother asked her and me to collect a few things from the garden. Her grief was a quickness in her movements, a brightness in her laughing, and I was instinctively uneasy when the side door closed behind us, leaving the two of us alone.

I suppose you're my guide, she said.

I guess, I said, trying not to sound as unhappy as I was.

She had been to the house every so often, always with her husband and sometimes with her daughter, Chie, whom I was friends with in the way that children are assumed to be friends with the children of their parents' friends. The husband, George, was the one out of the couple who was good with kids. He was sweaty and soft in a comforting way, and his joke most days at the start of a meal was to clasp his hands together and say: Dear God, thank you for these noodles. Ramen. He seemed to think there was something special about me that merited extra attention, which he would show by leaving the adults' table at some point in the evening to take me aside and ask me what I was reading or whether I had any girlfriends. Chie adored him. You could see it in her eyes, in the way you could tell where he was in the house at all times by the direction in which she refused to look.

Where George's attention was harmless and a little abject, Yukari's was severe and unpredictable. She always seemed to be on the verge of deciding I wasn't interesting enough to bother with. Last year, during the fall, she had yelled at a teacher in the parking lot after school and her voice had carried all the way through the fourth-floor windows to the classroom where I was playing the opening rounds of a schoolwide chess tournament. No one talked in the room. I didn't go to the window to see, and though the words were muddled by distance, I knew exactly whose voice it was. It went on and on. I didn't wonder about what was making her angry. Adults were mysteries to me then; their problems were unknowable. I remember only feeling sorry for Chie, that she had to live with a parent who was so capable of losing control.

A little later, Yukari and George had come over to the house at a strange time of day, midway between lunch and dinner. Yukari had walked with my mother to the park at the end of the street. George had gone upstairs to talk computers with my father. My father had been friends with George since he first arrived in Kyoto, and my mother with Yukari since before either of them were married. Their friendship had always been like this, always liable to break apart into their separate groups. I think each pair was prone to keeping secrets from the other, which was something my father would never have accepted with anyone except his oldest of friends, who had helped him at times when he believed he had no one else.

Now, outside in the garden, I walked Yukari along the fence to the far corner of the yard, where the green stems of the turnips were swaddled in straw. It was a cloudy day, and cold, and a north wind was skimming over our heads and rattling the dry leaves of the zelkova trees across the street.

Where's Chie? I said. Somehow it felt easier, out here in this maze of snow-bitten dirt, to talk to Yukari.

She's starting in a new school, she said. It's a boarding school. You can send letters if you want.

Where's Uncle George? I said.

She frowned. You're full of questions aren't you? she said. And then, as if to change the mood, she set her mouth in a line and asked, Do you wanna know a secret?

Okay.

They're talking about us, she said. In there. Your parents.

Why?

Because people always talk, she said. She laughed her tense, bright laugh.

A little later, she said, Okay, I lied. They're only talking about me.

She was kneeling on the ground. I hadn't noticed this before. Her feet were in the little path my mother had trampled into the soil, but one of her knees was in a section of green onions, another was crushing a white tent that covered a row of cauliflowers.

She cried a little then. In my mother's garden, between plots of winter vegetables, she cried quietly in a way that was almost impossible to tell. Then she stood up and brushed the dirt off her knees, but her jeans stayed gray and wet where the dirt had been, and on the hem of her blouse, where it had trailed on the ground.

Don't you dare tell anyone about this, okay? she said. She looked angry in a way that seemed to signal that we were both on the same side.

Okay, I said.

Good, she said. She wiped her cheeks, which were already dry. Her nose was red, but that could have been the cold.

On the way back to the house I could see my parents illuminated through the kitchen window: my father leaning back against the stove, my mother with her arms crossed at the sink. They were talking quickly about something, their heads bent, but I couldn't hear anything. At the side door, I thought Yukari lurched into the wall on purpose, making a dull thud, as if to let them know.

When we opened the door, my mother was arranging the fancy place settings at the table and my father was at the counter, mixing a vinaigrette. But the table was already laid out. My mother was only moving one green placemat a little to the left, and then back.

Suddenly, it was as though I could see that the whole house was grieving.

Where's Uncle George? I said. I needed to know. I was holding the turnips in a basket. They were heavy and cold. The smell of them, which was of winter and dirt, filled the kitchen. My father, who should have taken them from me, or told me to leave them in the sink, had his hands on the edge of the counter and his knuckles were white.

Where's Uncle George?

Much later, after George had been taken to court, after he reached a settlement with prosecutors, I heard that my father saw George one last time and asked him if he'd really done it. And when George stuck to the tired old story, that if he'd ever touched Chie in that way it had only been tickling, a sort of joke at most, my father waited a long moment, enough time for years to shift in his memory, for the world to rearrange itself into a different, more painful shape, before he helped his old friend pack the last of his things. But in the house with Yukari, when he was standing at the counter, he only turned sharply at my question, as if waking up from something, and said—Oh no, I wouldn't call him that—as if, for the first time, he could see a little of the structure of things.

Chie and George, 2015

He liked to say she was doppler-crying. In his telling, this was the point of the story, its beginning and its punchline. Crying so hard out the window, anyone on the sidewalk would have heard the two tones of her anguish, like an ambulance siren, as the car approached and drove away. She was that sort of child: histrionic, easily knocked sideways into tears or laughter. Her father liked to make fun of her for this, even now, after he was old and sick, after twenty years apart, the oxygen tank taking up room in his single-wide kitchen, behind his foldable chairs. He made the sound, like a race car, of her crying: *Eeeee-YOM*, the wind cutting through his teeth. He still laughed the same way, deeply, from the round bag of his belly. Back then, the car had been taking her to her mother's hotel room in the city, an early spat between her parents, when it still seemed that her family's problems were of the ordinary, forgivable kind. He was already hurting her then, she knew, but in little ways she would not recognize as hurt for years, not until it came rushing back to her after the court case, the therapy, like a wave overtopping a seawall, breaching the earth of a levee. *Eeeeee-YOM*. She had been a child who adored her father more than anything: more than truth, more than autonomy over her own body, more than her mother, whom she'd feared and hated that day in the car, as she was being driven to see her. Now, her dying father, making that noise through ruined lungs. He'd dragged her into the kitchen to tell her this story, had insisted on making her tea, wheezing over the Fig Newtons he scattered into a saucer with his shaking hands. She had agreed to see him only as a sort of experiment—you owe him nothing, a friend said—but she'd needed to compare the terror in her mind against the man. He was smaller than she remembered, and nervous in his little movements, in the way he kept gasping: *Eeee-YOM*. This was what he had left, she thought, of the father he could have been. And it was what she had left, she thought, of herself as his daughter, when she drove back through unfamiliar lanes, following the directions on her phone, merging onto the highway, rolling down the windows, feeling the wind on her shoulders, breathing the good, clean air.

Half-Blind

My friend is half dolphin, but he looks mostly human. In the right light, so long as he keeps his mouth shut, you would never know.

Lucky for you, I say. I try to imagine what would have happened to him otherwise. If he had flippers for arms, for instance, or just a trunk for legs.

Yeah, I got the good parts, he says, and then takes a breath so quickly it sounds like a snare drum. This is his habit. He can also hold his breath for twenty minutes straight.

Stop it, I say, twisting around furtively at the rest of the patrons in the streetside café. A few people are craning their heads curiously in our direction. One old lady shakes her husband's arm, trying to get his attention. I sigh as I turn to face my friend again. He laughs at me, his mouth hanging open, showing his conical teeth.

I'm half Japanese, which is not as big a deal as being half dolphin, but still, it's probably why we get along. I'm not saying that I choose all my friends that way, or that it defines me. I'm not even saying that it's all that different, being mixed. But I will say that from time to time it's nice to talk to someone who understands.

I got a call from my grandma, I'll say for example.

How did it go? my friend will say.

I still can't get her to believe that she's not being charged ten bucks a minute, I say. You know, overseas rates.

Ha! I can't even get mine to stop pressing the keypad during the call. I guess she just can't get over the sound it makes. But imagine you're trying to find out how her kidneys are holding up—you know, serious conversation—and you hear *beep!* and her voice says, What does that one do, Grandson?

I would hit my head against a wall, I say.

No, you'd yell, he says. You'd say, It does nothing, Grandma! You already made the call! The numbers are irrelevant now!

Except you don't, I say knowingly.

Yeah, I don't, he says.

Because it's already pretty impressive that your grandma learned how to use the phone at all, I say.

You're damned right it is.

One of the things I learn from him is that dolphins aren't as happy all the time as we think.

They sure look happy, I say.

That's just the way our jaws are made, he says. It'd be like if I thought the shape of your ears made you happy.

That would be pretty inconvenient.

It sure is.

How about Flipper? I say after a while. Wasn't he happy?

Oh God, he says. That's the most miserable dolphin you'll ever see.

Wow. That sure changes things.

You really couldn't tell? Those little noises he makes? The sad little way he twists his tail?

I ask about Flipper because it's my favorite movie. They played it once on TV in Japan when I was growing up. I remember turning around and seeing that odd look on my father's face. I think he'd grown up with it too, having lived for a while in Florida as a kid.

The look on his face convinced me to sit about a yard away from the screen and watch the whole thing through, almost without blinking. Then the next day I went to the video rental store, which was still a thing in those days, and went back home and we watched it again.

That's probably why I knew the first time I met my friend, even before he opened his mouth, that he was part dolphin. I knew it because he seemed like an old acquaintance, like somebody familiar from the far-off past.

Every Wednesday, during our lunch break, my friend and I go to the city pool. I'm a good swimmer. My father taught me himself. I always swim in the farthest right lane where all the kids who dropped out of the swim team, or the parents and grandparents who aged out, try to stay in touch with that part of their lives. My friend isn't much of a swimmer, but because he can hold his breath forever and also because his body sinks like a stone, he swims in the same lane as me, crawling slowly along the bottom of the pool where he's out of the way of everyone else. Strictly speaking, this isn't allowed, but the lifeguard on duty on Wednesdays is a friend of ours, and she understands.

Lately, though, he's started showing up with another friend who's part penguin, and this has become an issue.

The penguin friend can't swim fast and he can't sink either, although he, too, can hold his breath forever. His arms are perfectly serviceable flippers, but the rest of his body is too angular to glide easily through the water. He flounders across the pool like a broken paddleboat, making more waves than forward progress. Every other lap, I have to jump lanes to pass him. Sooner or later the lifeguard comes to the edge of the pool with an anxious look on her face.

He can't be here, she says to me.

That's Carl, I say. He's Edwin's friend.

He's getting in everyone's way, she says.

Carl comes over and tries to hang with his arms off the edge like I do, but he can't quite manage it. He slips off and bumps into a guy doing the butterfly. There's a slap and a splash that sends water across half the pool.

Put him in the slow lane, the lifeguard says.

C'mon, I say. Let him stay a little longer.

We used to swim an hour every week. After Carl joined, now we swim about fifteen minutes before we go to the changing room and watch the news on TV.

All Carl ever talks about is the ocean, and it gets on my nerves. He talks about overfishing and acidification, he talks about ocean politics and ocean history even, and I don't know how to talk about any of those things. Edwin knows though, of course, and when he's on that subject he turns into someone completely different.

My cousin's in Prague right now, Carl says. They're trying to renegotiate UNCLOS.

Really? says Edwin. How confident is he that they'll be able to change section 3.2?

You know the deal, says Carl. It seems like they might have a breakthrough, but then the Japanese won't put up with it.

The Japanese? I say.

The Japanese are kind of the Vladimir Putins of the maritime law world, says Edwin.

Exactly, says Carl. Wherever progress is about to be made, you can be sure they'll be there to stop it. Seriously, someone should figure out a way to just get rid of that entire nation.

Well, to be fair, says Edwin, most Japanese are fine.

Yeah? says Carl. Like which ones, exactly?

Like this one, says Edwin, and he puts a hand on my shoulder while Carl makes an awkward face. I try to smile back.

I appreciate Edwin's efforts, but somehow I get the feeling he only says that for my sake.

They say that in the land of the blind, the one-eyed man is king, but sometimes on my way back from the pool I wonder about the loneliness of that king. I wonder why he doesn't abdicate his throne and cross the border to the land of the one-eyed, where at least he fits in. I suppose it's possible there isn't such a land. Maybe the one-eyed people are stateless.

But still the king must keep close tabs on those who are at least partially sighted, on travelers from the land of the myopic, the republic of the cataract sufferers, and the farsighted and nearsighted too. Not out of a desire for conformity. Not because of some kind of nativism for the incompletely blind. But just because it's nice sometimes to be in a place where certain things don't have to be explained. Where you don't have to carry around the same stock answers to the same old questions and try to freshen them up each time you use them, try to pretend to even be interested in your own words.

So I've got my driver's test coming up, the king will say to his half-blind friends, and immediately they'll chime in: Good luck pal, those things are a nightmare! You used to be able to cheat by bringing glasses and secretly memorizing the order of the letters, but ever since they switched to those stupid little machines you peer into . . . I tell you what, though, if you're prepared to go a little out of your way, I know someone who works at the DMV who'll let you pass . . .

I run the scenario in my mind. I play out all the happy conversations, the comfortable adventures. But somehow by the time I reach my office again, it always ends up that even in the company of the partially sighted, the one-eyed man still feels alone.

Carl takes Edwin on a trip to see the sardine run in South Africa. They're gone for about a month, but it takes two more months after that before Edwin calls me.

Look, I say, before he has a chance to speak. We can all swim in the slow lane.

No, says Edwin. That's not a problem at all.

How was South Africa? I say.

It was great. We made friends with some seals. They're taking us to the movies tomorrow. You wanna come?

Can't, I say. I have a prior engagement.

What is it? he says.

Eye doctor, I lie.

Feel better, he says.

Which movie? I say, but the line has already gone dead. There's two quick beeps and then the sound of the wind, or maybe a long-held breath, thrumming down the wires, piling into my ears.

In the land of the blind and the one-eyed king, the eye doctor sits in his room, sharpening his knives and waiting for a call. Because he understands that the king can change himself. The king is lucky that way. He can be like everyone else if he wants. Over the years, in moments of sadness or weakness, how tempting that must be. How he must think about all the different, even painless ways to do it. In the quiet of the fading light at dusk, gazing out over the purple and orange sky, seeing the deep blue shadows creeping across his skin, dividing his face in half. Anesthetic and a knife, he must whisper to himself. Or a white-hot iron.

Maybe in the full light of day he understands that it would be a mistake. Maybe he reminds himself why he shouldn't do it. But at night, asleep in the pitch dark, the words come out and his hand creeps all by itself to the nightstand where the phone awaits.

Are you sure? says the eye doctor.

And the king, with his sleeping, greedy mind, breathes *Yes*.

My Father Will Not Admit He Has Become a Clown

Not even when he ties his clown-sized bowtie. Not even when he draws his clown-sized smile. Not even when he bends down to lace up his clown-sized shoes and then waves us goodbye with his clown-sized hands.

We have heard him on the train apologizing to a woman for touching her hair with his red-ball nose.

Maybe it is because we were slow to point it out. Maybe we gave him hope that we couldn't tell the difference. It takes us a long time to come up with the words to name it in a way that is not an accusation. A nice old woman, our neighbor, asks if he is available for hire as a "children's entertainer," and we decide we like the sound of this. But no, when we ask him, he will not even admit to this. This is on an evening when he comes home in the rain wearing pale makeup and a wig that is an afro in three different colors. We are worried that he is maybe about to start appropriating something. I make tea and my mother sits him down at the table. The tight whorls of his plastic hair flutter over his eyes when he shakes his head no.

For a whole month he drives to work with balloons and magic tricks packed in his briefcase. In the mornings he tells the joke about going to Subaru College, how he spends more hours in the hatchback than in the buildings of any campus. He teaches in Osaka on Tuesdays and Thursdays, in Kobe on Wednesdays, Kyoto on

Fridays. We are told that in class he juggles to the tune of our national anthem, which we find difficult to believe. Our national anthem is slow and somber, and we cannot imagine how he could keep the rubber balls in the air for long enough to hold time with the beat. We cannot imagine what his students are thinking, whether they applaud when he is done or resent him for wasting the time he should be using to pack their minds with foreign words.

In the second month we stage an intervention. This is with me, my mother, the nice neighbor, and the mean one, a professor of civil engineering who once, long before all this, in a dispute with us over ownership of the fence, had said my father had earned his degree from clown college. We remember this only when it is too late, after we have waved the neighbor through the door. My father had claimed that the fence was shared property and the neighbor had said this was impossible; later it emerged that my father had been right, but we understood that the dispute had been about something else. The property had been vacant for a long time before we moved in, and the neighbor had grown used to this. We were a swarm in the neighborhood, we were louder than silence, we took up too much of his space. We remember that the first time we met him, when we were heading to the park before touring the house, when we were just a family on a walk who could have been passing through from anywhere, he had smiled and been friendly, had looked up from working in the small raised beds of the garden in his yard and had offered us cherry tomatoes, boasting about their sweetness.

My father, when he shows up, seems unsurprised. He nods at each of us: my mother at the table, the mean neighbor on the sofa, the kind neighbor on a stool, and me standing against the wall. He hardly speaks much anymore, except to tell his jokes. Today he has little bells on his wrists that chime, and shoes that squeak.

What's the point? the mean neighbor says. He shakes his head. His arms are sprawled across the sofa cushions, taking up the whole thing. I don't see the damned point, he says.

Oh, oh, the nice neighbor says, a flutter in her throat. She gestures toward my mother, pats the air between them in the shape of an imaginary shoulder even though they are a good ten feet apart. Oh, she says. This seems to be the only thing she can think to say.

Dad, I say. We wanted to tell you something, I say.

I'm sorry, my mother says. This is something I don't expect her to say until she does. She says it with a straight back, her eyes fixed to the wall. Then she turns her gaze to my father with an effort, so you can see the tendons on the sides of her neck. I'm so sorry, she says.

Oh for Chrissakes, the mean neighbor says.

My father only smiles, but of course, it is painted on.

Later, when the neighbors have left and my parents think I have gone to my room, my mother cries in the kitchen and I see my father through the barely opened door, looking lost and confused and offering her a line of polka-dotted handkerchiefs, each a different color from the next.

We are told they are cutting staff at all his departments. That they are keeping only the young faculty, who are most energetic and personable and, most of all, cheaper. Of course we are worried about this, but there is nothing we can do. My mother asks her old friends about job openings in the big companies downtown. My mother is a receptionist at a school for the blind, a job she chose because she likes the people she works with and the mission of the place, even though it pays less than it could. She would hate a downtown office, but it would cover some expenses, she says.

My father doesn't seem to know. He goes to work at the same time every day as always. Some days he pins a clover to his breast pocket. Some days he carries a wand.

If he cursed or cried it would be less worrying. What is worrying is to wake up to silence in the middle of the night.

The nice neighbor is the one who offers us statistics: crime rates, cancer risks, life expectancies. You can never be too careful, she says. It seems the future of a clown is uncertain at best.

We never knew. The disaster we were courting. The things we should have seen, but ignored.

Helium: in its own way, a loaded gun.

This is a problem we can solve. It isn't even very difficult. One day, while he is down at the store, we drag the heavy metal tanks out of the trunk of his car. We fill the whole house with balloons and watch them bobble out of reach. In every room a different color, nosing the rafters. When my father finally comes back, a ripple goes through them with the *snick-snick* of rubber on rubber, so that they crest in a wave from the front door to the living room and back again.

Isn't this something? my father says. This is the first thing he has said in weeks. He sets down the groceries and looks up at the ceiling.

Yes, my mother says, and I see it too.

In a small way, it's a different world. It changes the sound of everything. And in the evening—when the ceiling lights cast a sort of magic on the walls, and the colors bleed and drift like clouds. And later, when the balloons are shriveled cats in the corners of the rooms. That is something too.

The day my father gets fired from the last of his jobs, he doesn't come home for hours, and then when he does he is wet and shivering like a foal. Outside, in his car, his huge shoes are abandoned in the trunk and filled with river stones. My mother is out searching for him in the city until she calls from a payphone inside the liquor store where he sometimes goes. Keep him there, she says over the phone. Don't let him out of your sight.

She takes the downtown office job. My father sleeps for days. After a long time, ten days, he steps out of bed in his old fleece sweater and rumpled pajama pants and stumbles downstairs.

Okay, he says. I am ready for the world.

And he is.

2

きのう召されたタコ八は
弾丸にあたって名誉の戦死
タコの遺骨はいつかえる
骨がないのでかえれない
タコの母ちゃん寂しかろ

Conscripted only yesterday, Octopus
takes a bullet and dies a hero's death.
When will his bones come home?
They can't come home; he has no bones.
His mother must be lonely.

—From a popular wartime song (author unknown)

たこが海で死んだ。何にも悲しいことはない

An octopus died in the sea.
There's nothing to grieve.

—Morita Kazuyoshi, speaking on the drowning of his friend Saitō Seisaku, better known as Octopus Hachirō

The Mystery of Animal Grief

Of course there are elephants who mourn their dead. And whales that lift their stillborn children to the surface to breathe. And in Japan, where I grew up, it seemed that every town had a dog memorialized in a statue, movie, or book. One dog swam to an island each morning to meet its partner. Another ran to a station each evening to meet its owner. And always, like an epilogue, the bittersweet ever-after of the canine fairy tale: how the partner died, or the owner did, but every day that dog would make the trip just the same.

But the one that gets me most is the one I'm not even sure is true. This is the one about the dolphin fish, and how fishermen will tell you, when you hook one, to always try to get another. The idea is that they live in pairs and the surviving fish gets lonely. It tries to find its mate. And I have once seen a dolphin fish swim stubborn circles around our boat while its husband, flushed with gold and emerald, made beautiful by fright, pumped its blood onto the deck. And afterward every tossed piece of bait bringing this fish to the surface, shimmying its flanks against a slice of minnow, a herring, as if touch were the only thing. As if it didn't care to see.

What draws me to this story is the incongruity of it: the idea of a grieving fish, inconsolable, snacking on a passing lure. And what repels me from this story is what it thinks I will believe: that a dolphin fish, facing loss, discovers the hook.

Nishina Sekio in a Tunnel Alone

There are spots of silver eating through his vision and it's hard to see through them. They crawl across his eyes like fat worms, shimmering like molten lead. The more they eat, the bigger they become. Already there are only a few patches where he can see.

He shakes his head but he can't dislodge the worms. Somehow he doesn't think to raise his hands to wipe them from his eyes.

There's someone sitting on the gyroscope. This is what he thinks. He thinks that maybe he can see a foot there and one square shoulder beside an angular head. He needs to know because the gyroscope is very important and it might not work if someone is sitting on it. This is why, even though he has hardly a breath to spare, he calls out to it.

Kuroki, he says. Kuroki, is that you?

Nishina, you son of a bitch, says a voice, and he knows from the words that it must be him.

I'm glad you're here, says Nishina. I couldn't tell. It's hard to see.

Of course it is, says Kuroki. You're sucking on kerosene fumes.

Ah, says Nishina. That's right. I forgot about the fumes.

How could you forget? The engine is right behind your head.

Nishina remembers with an effort about the engine. He hears the roar of it behind him, or he thinks he does, although the sound seems oddly muted as though it's coming from behind a damp towel. He tries to see if he can smell it, that smell of soot and burning oil, and that's when he remembers that it's been a long time since he last took a breath.

Breathe, says Kuroki.

Right, says Nishina. He tries to breathe, but he's not sure if he's doing it. His body is a fuse box where someone has peeled off all the labels. He can flip the switches but he has no idea where each one is connected. He tries something and he feels the muscles in his neck tense up. He tries something else and it clenches his back.

It's no use, says Nishina.

It's too late, says Kuroki. Carbon monoxide, you know.

Shit. So this is what it's like.

Be happy. You have it better than I did. I got carbon *dioxide*, remember? That was much more work.

But Nishina doesn't remember. He sits silently for a while, waiting for the worms to crawl out of his sight. The engine is behind him, he remembers. On either side of him are the narrow walls of a tunnel. In front of him is the butt of a black steel tank. He has to squint to see, because even the parts without the worms are getting darker now, as if the light is beginning to fade.

Kuroki, are you sitting on the gyroscope?

No. I'm on the stopwatch.

Ah, says Nishina. He forgot about the stopwatch too. The stopwatch is set to five minutes and it's counting down to zero. He can't remember what happens when it runs out.

Don't worry about it, says Kuroki. That's one thing you don't have to worry about.

Good, says Nishina. I have enough worry as it is. It's good that you're here to tell me about the things I don't have to worry about.

Nishina thinks that it's getting hot inside the tunnel, or maybe it was always this hot and he's only just now noticing it. He can taste the saltiness of the sweat in his mouth even though he can't feel the dampness of it on his skin. He can taste the oil in the air, too, and he thinks he can see it, little floating droplets moving past his face. It's as though the air itself were a sponge and kerosene were being wrung out of it.

Why are we in a tunnel, Kuroki?

Kuroki starts to laugh. It's a wheezing, coughing sound and partway through, Nishina hears something slide across the floor.

You think we're in a tunnel? says Kuroki. You, of all people. I really thought you would know.

Know what?

You don't remember anything, do you?

I'm trying, Kuroki.

Nishina feels something pressed against the top of his head and he tries to think of what it is. A periscope, he thinks, the word coming to him slowly, one syllable at a time—*per-i-scope*. A little baby of a thing, he remembers. The damnedest contraption. It had been almost impossible to see out of. Like looking through the wrong end of toy binoculars. It folds up, he remembers, just like toy binoculars, and through it he had seen . . . He can't remember what he had seen.

Our little invention, says Kuroki. We spent such a long time on it.

Nishina tries to shake his head but the wires that are all crossed up in his body make him wiggle his elbows instead. So he tries to speak. His voice is small now, and his mouth is dry, but still he manages to make a little noise.

Kuroki.

Outside the walls of the tunnel Nishina can hear something, or maybe he feels something. A distant shaking. A series of impacts. One of them shakes his hand so that it falls from his lap. He tries to pick it up but he can't move it.

Help me Kuroki.

Nishina hears a long, exasperated sigh as a small white box slides into view. It looks strangely familiar but he can't remember where it's from. It comes to rest against one of his boots. It looks like an urn, he thinks, but he doesn't know why he thinks this.

We believed in this, says the box. You and I, we believed in this together. Even after my silly accident, stuck in the muck. Don't you remember?

The engine grates against his head like a drill pounding into rock.

There are so many dials in front of him, so many sharp edges. He remembers Kuroki, his smooth chin, his double joints, how he'd used to be able to touch the inside of his wrists with the fingers of his same hand. How he'd had narrow shoulders—a submariner's shoulders, Kuroki would say, squeezing onto a crowded bench outside the mess hall, watching the waves come in. He had eyes that could catch the light in any weather. His sneezes only ever came in groups of three. He could show you eight different swells on a given day, tell you their individual directions, sing out their separate rhythms. It was something about the spacing and distance, he remembers, though he can't remember exactly what. Something about those two things, and you could guess where it had come from. You could smoke and tell stories and imagine gales over Java, rain falling on Palau, thunderheads skimming the mountains of New Guinea, sliding down rugged cliffs, the sun tilting into the sea, the light fading, just as it is now, Nishina's vision going yellow, then gray, then blue.

I wrote you a letter in the dark, the box says. You paced the dock all night, thinking of ways to save me. Someone made a speech, a beautiful speech, about rowboats following each other through the teeth of a storm. You asked to see my body when they cut me from the wreck.

Nishina doesn't remember. Try as he might, he can't recall a thing. All he knows is that the shaking is getting stronger and he has a vague worry about the stopwatch. He wants to know how much time is left on it but he doesn't think Kuroki will tell him. Kuroki, who is in a box. In a box in a tunnel. And Nishina is trapped in here with him. He doesn't think he has enough strength left to ask many other questions. He settles for the one that's most on his mind.

Kuroki, what am I doing here?

The box is silent for a long time, and then, as the shaking stops, Nishina hears it clear its throat.

You're dying for your country, it says. That's what this is.

Nishina wants to know more, but the stopwatch tells him that he's out of time.

Preparations, 2015

Seventy years after the war is over and here is my mother, taping white crosses to the windows against the bombardment of a storm that threatens to settle in the hollow of her yard. Plywood is better, is what I could have told her if I had been there to say it. My mother with her straw hat, her elbow-length gloves stained in the crooks of the fingers by the loam of the garden, and my father with his bad back at the base of the ladder, braced against a wind that hasn't yet come. Maybe there's no stopping the memories that push through the dirt like amber cicadas waking as one from a long and troubled sleep. Maybe there's nothing I could have said to my mother on that ladder, who turns from the window and sees her whole life spread out before her. The neighbors with their children throwing crazy streamers of masking tape to each other across the gravel of their driveway. The old man down the block who is stringing the curtains closed on the window over the sink of his kitchen, who is filling metal buckets that must be a thousand years old with a hose that he snakes through the gap in his cobwebbed door. And here is my grandmother, unbidden, who closes her invisible hands over my mother's eyes, who lets her warm breath heave into her ears with the knowledge of the sirens that rang and rang, even when the bombs were falling, even when the fires were twining up the street and wavering the patterns on the crisscrossed glass that was meant to hold the world at bay.

It's my father, in the end, with his anxious eyes, who peers up at my mother against the ceiling of clouds and reaches his hand to the skin of one ankle where her pants have ridden past the hem of her blood-pressure socks.

That's enough, is what he says in the only voice that cuts through the haze of her thoughts, and she climbs down the ladder with her blind toes seeking the rungs, until my father pats the dust off the backs of her shoulders and they stand for a spell with their arms at their hips, watching the storm roll in and in and the tumbling wind that hauls grit from the soil and sets it rising and rising until it turns to smoke, to light.

Home Burial

Yashima Nobuaki died alone. Nobody liked him much, except his daughter, who of course was obliged. He was the sort of old man you might not see in town for years at a time except occasionally, by the road, trimming the camellia bushes at the edge of his property or lecturing some poor kid for climbing the fence. Other than family, only my grandmother went to his wake. Out of a sort of professional courtesy, my mother said. My grandmother had suffered a stroke that spring, and she was driven there and back by my mother, who had to place a stepstool on the driveway and guide her by her elbows into the back of the van. My grandmother wore a black kimono with a white and gold sash. I had never seen her dressed up before.

Years ago, in the war, she worked for Yashima in the village hall. This was after she fled Osaka with her mother after they lost the house. The summer of 1945. She was fifteen years old. Yashima's job was to recommend men in the village for the draft. My grandmother was the one who locked the pale red draft letters into a metal box on the back of a bicycle and delivered them one by one to each house.

A killer behind a desk, my grandfather said. He should have been strung up like a murderer.

This was after my mother had left with the van. He sat in the mudroom and let his fingers wander over the top of the bench. He used to smoke all the time but stopped cold about a week after my grandmother's stroke. Having to leave the hospital room, I think, was part of what made him stop. We'd been on his case about it for years, but never thought he would do it. Sometimes, when he's feeling down, you can still see that he misses it, having something in his hands. In these moments he looks very old, even older than he is.

I heard it described this way, some time ago, by a stranger. An old friend of someone in town, she had tea with practically everyone and then left again for good. Your grandma was a cog, she said, a little girl. But old man Yashima could have lied. He could have protected someone.

My grandmother comes home early the next morning and sits in the mudroom with her head very still. It's a while before I realize she's drunk, the way she speaks very little and doesn't want to be helped into her room to change. You smell of onions, my mother says, helping her pull off her sandals. My grandfather, looking startled, says: It was a wake, of course she drank. My grandmother is dignified, holding herself in, steadying herself against fixed objects with her hands. Ever since her stroke, when she lost fine motor control on most of her left side, she tends to sit with her right shoulder raised slightly above her left, as if warding off some threat that is always in her peripheral vision. It's the beginning of January, and the blood seeps slowly back into her ears, over the crests of her cheekbones, around the base of her nose.

Of course I drank, she says. She forms the words carefully, her voice strangely loud. There are goosebumps on her wrists, over her very white knuckles.

You're freezing, my mother says, let's get you into the house. But my grandmother doesn't move, refuses to be pulled up by her arms.

Toshio, she says, using my grandfather's first name. Ordinarily they call each other "you" with a kind of gruff affection, but this is more direct, a question from a different time. Will you go to the funeral?

My grandfather, looking away, shakes his head.

And you? to my mother, who is still standing above her.

Come get some sleep, my mother says. I'll wake you in a few hours.

You? My grandmother looks to me.

Yes, Grandma, I tell her. Mom and I are both going.

Good, she says.

After she leaves I find my grandfather in the hallway, staring at nothing on the walls. Behind him, my grandmother has shut the door to their room. They aren't showy in love, but love deeply, I think. The way he shadows her, within earshot, even through the closed door. The way she will sometimes laugh around the dinner table at a joke he hasn't yet said aloud. Back in May, when a blood vessel burst in her brain and flushed her eyes red, my grandmother spent two hours flat on the ground feeling spit slide down her cheek and puddle into her hair. The neighbors were out working and there was no one around. Halfway up the mountain, a little past noon, my grandfather, tending to the farthest plot in their orchard, put down his tools and came home early. He searched everywhere trying to find her. No one else could have saved her life.

In this town, even now, they only do home burials. It's the sort of place where you might stumble onto a gravestone in the woods, or spot one through a car window in the middle of rice fields on its own little rectangle of grass. Of course, you can tell the soldiers apart from the date of death. My grandparents' family grave is fifty yards downhill from the house, between an empty barn and a ditch that marks the edge of the neighbor's property. In May it is buried in wild azaleas, in winter, snow. There are eight or nine relatives named there and two brothers, each a few years older than my grandfather, who died in '45 when they were seventeen and nineteen years old. This is where my grandmother was, and where my grandfather found her, moving as fast as his brittle legs could take him, and saved her.

It was an accident, is what I've heard—in the war, why they asked my grandmother to do it. The winter of 1945 was long and cold, with puddles freezing overnight late into the spring. Yashima, delivering the draft by bicycle, was the only one using the roads at night, and nobody could warn him of where there was ice ahead. At the beginning of April, when he crashed into a ditch, he snapped two ligaments in his knee and could hardly stand up, even with crutches. Ordinarily it would have been a man who filled in for Yashima, but in the middle of planting season, in the last year of the war, there were none to spare. Yashima would be the brains, my grandmother his legs, making the trips he could not. A city girl, they must have figured hers was a labor they could afford to lose. As for her, she just wanted to be useful. Moving from Osaka to this tiny village, running from bombs, she needed to get by.

So much was asked of her. The draft letters that always arrived at the village hall in the middle of the night. The death notices that arrived by day. This was the year that boys as young as fifteen were allowed to enlist. One of Yashima's jobs was to convince them. Fifteen years old—the same age as my grandmother. She was in work groups with their sisters, in their front yards chatting with their aunts and mothers. She walked them down to Yashima's office, and watched them walk out, would have seen their eyes filled with dread and hope.

This much is certain: if my grandmother and Yashima had tried less hard, fewer people would have died. Or if they died anyway, they would have come from someplace else.

My mother and I go home to Kyoto two days after the funeral, promising to come back soon. This is how it is; years go by like this. My mother visits most often, on holidays or sometimes for the weekend, driving or taking the expressway bus five hours one way. My father and I go with her, or don't. It's a whole town of old people now, 二ちゃん農業 (grandparent farming) is what it's called, how they seem to be stranded in the past, how one orchard after another shuts down as the nursing homes in the nearest city fill up. In little ways here and there you can see how the seams pull apart. On our way out of town, at the bottom of the valley, we pass Yashima's old house. The front doors have been left wide open, his daughter must be out, and there is no one inside. My mother pulls the car over and I get out, let myself in through the gate. Yashima's front doors are weather-beaten wood with glass panes that rattle in the wind. They must have been left open overnight, and no one has noticed. In the mudroom there is frost weaving itself across floor tiles and a small wooden tabletop; a mound of cashews abandoned in an ashtray; one cup, bathringed with old tea, left on a coaster.

Years go by.

My grandfather finally sells the orchard, and he seems lost without it. His hair, which had stayed black into his seventies, whitens in the space between one visit and the next, and for one whole second, across the distance of the driveway, when he opens the door, I don't know who he is. The next winter, my grandmother falls on her bad arm as she's pulling herself to the bathroom in the middle of the night. She needs two months in the hospital, and then, near the end of her stay, working herself along handrails in the corridor outside her room, she loses her grip and fractures a rib. I love the food too much, is the joke she chooses to tell; I couldn't bear the thought of going out into the world and tasting salt again. In the summer I leave for college and my parents grow older through my computer screen. In the fall I am neck-deep in exams, hardly seeing the sun, calling no one. My first winter back, after unpacking my things, I make the drive out alone to my grandparents' house.

It's early January, my parents are already back at work, and I am looking for something to do. I borrow their old Gemini and stuff the hatchback full of junk food and clothes. A long, slow drive, and I am standing in the shadow of persimmon trees, looking up at the lights shining through the pebbled glass of my grandparents' kitchen windows.

Look at you, my grandfather says, when I walk through the door.

The prodigal grandson, my grandmother says, beaming. She is wheelchair-bound now, but talks tough as ever. She makes a production out of ordering my grandfather around, pointing to things on high shelves and sometimes, at the last moment, changing her mind. My grandfather submits to most of this cheerfully, though from time to time a mood will close over him and he will refuse to hear a thing she says. Tomorrow I am driving her to Yashima's old place for his 三年祭 (the third anniversary of his death). This is part of why I'm here. When I called to say I was making the trip, my grandmother grabbed the phone and asked if I could do it two days earlier. My mother, who drove her to the fiftieth- and hundredth-day ceremonies and the first anniversary, warned me to prepare for shouting. My grandfather refuses to go or even to drive her, and the fighting gets worse every time. She accuses him of being heartless, my mother tells me, and childish. And then he blames her for wanting to get drunk in public. I guess this is the easy response, the one that comes first to mind and slips out when he's not expecting it, and that must hurt them both when it does.

Over dinner, while my grandfather is changing the channel on the little TV, my grandmother says: our grandson drove five hours just to take me fifteen minutes down the road.

He's a young man, my grandfather says. What's the problem? He loves driving.

Later, he says: Why would anyone feel bad for that guy?

This is during the seven o'clock news. The camera crew is on location outside the home of a disgraced pop star. From the far side of the road a small group of his fans are chanting and holding signs to show their support.

My grandmother, turning to me: Your grandpa would send us all to hell if he could.

My grandfather, to her: And you would have us go to all the funerals.

Oh Toshio, she says, you don't know what you've said.

On the news, the fans are chanting—Stay strong, Stay strong—and the reporters are recounting his crimes.

Would you send me to hell, Toshio? my grandmother says. Would you do that?

I've had about enough of this, my grandfather says. He looks stricken, how he fumbles his arms through his coat sleeves, how slowly he walks into the hall. My grandmother doesn't move her gaze from her lap. The kitchen door slides open, and then closed.

I've never heard my grandfather talk about his brothers. But I know that their graves are empty. They came home in 1946 in two wooden boxes, each about the size of a head. Inside, there were papers with their dates of death, their final ranks in the army. But of their bodies there was not even a hair or a tooth—there was nothing but air.

They would have still held a full funeral. The priest would have blessed an empty box. Someone, maybe my grandfather, would have walked at the head of the procession with an empty urn in his arms. They would have buried the emptiness, which is the sort of thing, I think, that must be ignored and confronted, confronted and ignored, and never dies.

My grandfather is gone the next morning. When I wake up, I walk through the whole house looking for him. My grandmother, who acts as though nothing is wrong, combs the knots out of her hair, tells me which things to pack in her bag. In the driveway, when I have to lift her from the wheelchair, I stop.

What's wrong? she says.

I don't know if I'm macho enough, I say, and she laughs, but I can see it's forced, how she recognizes the exaggeration and, a second later, tells her muscles to move.

Lift me up kiddo, she says, and I do.

I take her to Yashima's. The drive feels almost instantaneous: the bright sun, the bare branches of the persimmon trees flitting past, the high mountain ridges above the valley on either side. Two hours later, I pick her up again. There's no one on the road, no one parked in front except the priest who has come up from the city. There should be a group of mourners, some friends and relatives, I'd thought. I had imagined that someone, in all these years, would have forgiven him. The house looks the same as ever, nothing has changed, except my grandmother waiting on the asphalt, who cannot hide the exhaustion in her face.

Look at me, she says, can't make it through the days. In the back seat, after I settle her in, she holds one hand over her eyes, lets it slide to her chin. A minute later, pulling out of the first turn in the road, I hear it thunk into her lap.

She sleeps.

In the rearview mirror she is a ghost of herself. She looks pale in the mottled light, and afraid in a way she will never let herself look while awake. I asked my mother once what had brought my grandparents together and she said she thought it was safety—how my grandmother arrived in the village after having nearly died in the city, bombs crashing down around her, and decided to marry the most dependable man for miles around—and for my grandfather, possibility—how years after the war, in the new world that seemed to be beginning, my grandfather chose the one woman he could find who knew what it was like to leave a place. It could have ended them, these different needs, each misunderstanding the other, but there was something about their patience for each other that made it work. In my grandparents' bedroom there is a conch shell from Hawai'i, a diorama from Vietnam, and a fur hat from Kamchatka; they really did leave, in their fifties and sixties, if only for a little while each time, my grandfather wide-eyed, holding the camera, my grandmother obliging, pulling their bags behind. And each time they came home to the safety they had built together, the dependable persimmon trees, how they had put up half the buildings on the property themselves, starting from dragging logs up the mountain, the way my grandfather could rustle up friends to help him in anything, in shaving bark off the pillars of their house, in raising them true. It must be that they have had to hold so much that seems contradictory in their minds for so long, having been kids in the war, and through the end of it, and the famine that followed, and the boom years after that, how they can gauge things in two ways, even when it comes to Yashima: the fact that my grandfather has always blamed and not blamed my grandmother, and that she blames and forgives herself.

All these decades, and my grandmother has always been the one to tidy up the family grave, even on the day of her stroke.

Halfway up the road we pass under a highway bypass that the prefecture is constructing over the valley. In a few years strangers in fast cars will be able to look out over the town on their way between two minor cities and notice the houses dwindling, farms turning to brush, the whole place swallowed up, bit by bit, by trees. For now the two halves of the bridge are bone-white fingers pointing from the hillsides to the places in midair where they will someday meet. There must be ice on the concrete, how the bottom edge of it is lacquered in the sun, a silver knife. The road is winter-white, then shadowed, then bright. At the top of the road I turn off into my grandparents' drive.

I help my grandmother into the house. I walk through the rooms. On the phone, by the bottom of the stairs, my mother tells me to wait. Trust me, she says, he always comes back.

Always? I say.

Don't worry, she says.

And she's right: I wait and wait, and he comes home at six, just before dark.

We are sitting in the dining room. My grandmother is trying her best to laugh and I am trying my best to make her. The kitchen door rattles open, and my grandfather walks into the hall. He unlaces his boots. He takes off his coat. He must be cold: in the kitchen, he puts the kettle on. In the dining room, he pulls up a chair.

Mutsuko, he says, I wouldn't send you to hell.

That's it? she says.

That's it, he says.

Okay, she says.

Okay.

When the kettle boils, he gets up. He comes back with tea for all of us.

Housefire

On the day my grandmother started a fire in the kitchen, she talked of holding, which she had been doing for some time. The morning after New Year's, and the dispatcher asked my mother if she was sure it was an emergency; the fire station was shorthanded, and the address my mother gave was at least half an hour away. My grandmother sat in her wheelchair and played with the snow under her slippers. She clicked her false front teeth in and out of her mouth. When I tried to flag down the fire engine from the nearest road, she hugged me and wouldn't let go.

On the day my grandmother started a fire, she talked of holding, and had been doing so for some time. She had turned eighty-two in June and developed a habit of launching into sentences that seemed untethered from anything that had gone before. For about a year she talked of the importance of holding. The left side of her body had been debilitated by a stroke some time before and was wasted and thin. Until then she had worked a farm her whole adult life. On some days the right side of her body contained incredible strength; on others she was helpless. It was hard to say what accounted for the difference. She could move her left arm but had no strength in the hand, couldn't lift anything with it. She liked to make a joke of it, called it ダメ田・ダメ太郎 (Dameda Damedarō), a name like Baddy

McBadface, gave it a voice, a child's whine, when she would lecture it on the need for grip, the importance of holding. Five years ago she was cabled in muscle, drove crated cucumbers and dried persimmons in the back of her white van down mountain roads in every weather, taking the banked corners like a race car driver, hardly slowing down.

On the day my grandmother started a fire in the kitchen, the dispatcher asked my mother if she was sure it was an emergency. The smoke started when a pot boiled down to nothing and sparked into flame. Soon it was in the grease cladding the ceiling and the tops of the walls and there was nothing to be done. The kitchen had been recently remodeled, but the house was older than my mother and there were no alarms. It was the morning after New Year's and my grandmother had wanted to make お雑煮, a sweet soup that had been my favorite as a child of three or four. We'd started buying fancy crates of premade おせち ever since my grandmother's stroke. The food was for New Year's but the leftovers often lasted for days.

The prospect of an accident at the house had loomed like smoke over this arrangement for years, the question of how long my grandparents could last in this farmhouse on their own, the home health aides that insurance paid for three days a week, the neighbors who left gifts of leftover stew on the doorstep, how we lived so far away and could visit only so often, the danger we studiously ignored. Out in the snow, as we watched smoke pour from the windows, the kitchen lit from inside like a lantern, I realized that my grandmother had lost her tether in time, that her strange asides were missives from years I didn't know. We waited for what felt like hours for the fire engine to come, but it was only thirty minutes. From time to time neighbors came by to stare mutely at the house, and couldn't seem to leave.

On the day my grandmother sparked fire, she had been talking of holding for some time, maybe about a year. She had turned eighty-two and developed a habit of launching into sentences that seemed untethered from anything that had gone before. She said that a child of three or four must be held against the chest, never led by the hand. She inserted this information into conversations about groceries, the progress of the bypass construction over the valley, the unending hold of the Liberal Democratic Party over national politics. She categorized the drones of various taxi engines, semi-trucks, bullet trains on TV by aircraft type. Sikorsky. Mustang. B-29 but flying high, unloaded. In a crowd, if you lead a child by the hand, when people pack so close together it hurts, you'll be forced to lose them. This is what she said. Even bones burn blue, so from a distance you'll know. In cars, in supermarket parking lots, my parents had started discussing an arrangement that my mother insisting on calling "apartment living": a building in the nearest city where every bed had an alarm button and nurses would check in at least twice a day.

She wanted to make お雑煮 in the morning as a way of proving she was still capable, that she was worthy of independence. She shooed us out of the kitchen when we offered to help. The kitchen had been recently remodeled with a raised floor so she could sit in her wheelchair and still see into the pot, but the walls and ceiling were older than my mother and there were no alarms. Where my grandparents live the お雑煮 is a sweet soup with mochi and a base of azuki beans. The beans have to be boiled for almost two hours. Maybe she lost those hours, or added too little water, or maybe she forgot to add any water at all.

My grandmother on the day sparked fire in the kitchen for some time, maybe hours. She was eighty-two and untethered from years: on some days she was as strong as anyone, on others was lost. There was no accounting for the difference. In her youth she coiled red ropes around her back and arms and sang work songs in the mud, plunged seedlings in neat rows with her cloth-covered hands. The songs were about the old myths of a time when the land was dew falling to the ocean off the point of a spear. Before that she was a child in Osaka running from flames, had lived in mud atop the embers of her house in a neighborhood flattened by bombs. After that she fled to farmland. She developed a habit of unhooking her front teeth from her mouth in moments of anxiousness. They were a bridge and never seemed to fit right. She had operated the winch when my grandparents pulled raw lumber up the mountain to build the farmhouse, before my mother was born. A steel hook had come untethered from bark and snapped the coiled cable like a whip. She lost three teeth and bled all over the back of a motorcycle on the long ride to the hospital. She liked to make a joke of the false set, called them ダメ田・ダメ太郎 (Dameda Damedarō), a name like Baddy McBadface, gave them a voice, a child's whine, in her grip.

On the day my grandmother started a fire in the kitchen she talked of holding, a real emergency, until there was nothing to be done. The fire station was shorthanded, and the address my mother gave was at least half an hour away. We smelled the sugar burning, and then the grease. We found my grandmother in the bathroom at the other end of the hall. Outside, the neighbors crowded and crowded in around us. My grandmother sat in her wheelchair and played with the snow under her slippers. Her mood was untethered like a child's. After what felt like hours, but was only thirty minutes, the fire truck climbed the nearest road, its engine droning, under heavy load. The flashing lights turned the house red, then white. I tried to meet it, but my grandmother hugged me and wouldn't let go. A child of three or four, she said. The child was her. Her eyes were terror. Her hands were hooks. There was nothing to be done. The past gripped her, and then released her.

I know I can't live out here, she said, her slippers in snow. She was as strong as anyone.

Suicide Drills, 1945

The rag is meant to be a grenade. Nobody explains this to us, but it becomes clear sooner or later. Our teachers hand us each a balled-up rag and tell us, more or less, to sprint into the sandbox and throw our bodies on top of it. The instructions are complicated but the meaning comes through simply, for each of us, at different times. The fourth-grade class of Iya Elementary. Fifteen nine-year-olds. Boys and girls. A boy has his face in the sand when he thinks, *Oh, I get it, this is a grenade*. A girl is lifting her face too early—stay down ten seconds, or start again—when she thinks, *a grenade*. A boy is feeling a teacher kick the small of his back into the ground with a foot—stay down, dammit—when he thinks, *grenade*.

A long day. Grains of sand in our eyebrows. In the washboards of our shins. The next day, at school, seeing rags in a bucket, in the back of a closet, we think, *Those aren't grenades, but*—looking at the teacher, our classmates, our houses on the hill—*we are weapons*; and we are awed by this knowledge, hard won.

Later that day, the weapons of the U.S. Navy fly over our village on their way to bomb the weapons of houses and schoolyards in the city by the sea. We watch them glide over treetops, the long silver flecks, fading toward the horizon like stars.

The Grandma Invasion

My grandmother turns cancerous. She multiplies in her bed. Before you know it she's in every room: trailing a hundred different IVs, a hundred different threadbare slippers.

The slippers. grandmothers one through thirty are mesmerized by slippers. At the end of each hall is a machine that chews them up and spits them out. Put your old ones on top and in a moment a new pair whizz-clicks out the bottom. Hot pink slippers slip-slapping the linoleum. I don't know why every grandmother wears a different color: Blue-Brown Slippers Grandma, Gray-Green Slippers Grandma, the one grandma whose slippers are cast-iron black.

Some grandmothers do better than others. One has enough grip strength to chop her own hangnails. One doesn't need a swan potty by her bed. There's Escapee Grandma, who sometimes makes it all the way to the stairs. There's Crafty Grandma, who folds things out of glossy paper from the magazines: potholders, tea cozies—the peony beside her bed has some singer's laced thighs all over the face of it.

Grandmothers four through forty hate TV but watch it anyway. Grandmothers nineteen through ninety can't stand the way the nurses try to style their hair. Grandmothers fifty through fifty-five want to know if I'll be back tomorrow. Grandmothers sixty-three to seventy hope I come bearing gifts. Grandmothers seventy-two to a hundred wish I'd stay away.

Their scalps are dry like wax paper in an oven but their lungs hold water like baobab trees. Grandmothers four through twelve chuckle they'd be useful in a desert. You could carry me like a coconut, says grandmother thirty-five. They each get suctioned dry every week: a big breathing machine that puff-puffs their water out. Afterward, with Marlboro throats Grandmothers eighteen through twenty-four want to know where the nurses are taking it. Grandmother twenty-five thinks it goes in her soup. Grandmother thirty-eight wants a little break before the next time. Go easy on the bilge, she says, I'm not a boat, you know.

Clingy Grandma can't sleep without a hand to hold. The trick is to wait to loosen her grip. Child, she slumbers, if I start too soon. Don't you remember the blankets I made? Don't you remember needing me?

I'm sorry, she says, suddenly afraid-awake.

Drive safe, says Sensible Grandma, waving me off.

You bastard, says Scary Grandma, hissing through her dentures.

I say: it's late—backing away, away.

Grandmothers one through eighty plead: take me home for the holidays. Grandmothers one to sixty get rejected in writing. Grandmothers sixty-one through eighty-five receive their answers in person. Crafty Grandma wakes from a nap to find her bribe of ten potholders returned to a pile by her bed.

On New Year's Day, Escapee Grandma misses the third step, and the hospital goes dark. I arrive in the getaway van, twenty minutes too late. The technicians lay a cloth over their coconut heads. They stuff the grandmas in the furnace, all in a line, and when they're done, only a jar-full of bones comes out.

We Are a Woman Bombed / A Picture of Grace

We are a woman bombed.

We are bombed as a child. The bomb makes us sick.

We are sick with the bomb.

Later, when we are healed, other people believe we are sick.

This is when we are older. When we find our first job. When we try to get married. When we want our first child.

People think the sickness we have is catching.

They are sorry for us, and afraid of us. We are also afraid.

We are afraid for our life, and for those of others, and for that of our child. We are afraid for our fear. There is too much in our lives for us to fear.

One day, after many years, the leader of the country that made the bomb comes to our city. It is a big event. It is in the news for weeks.

He is coming to talk to the bombed people, we hear.

He has many things to say. After all this time. Nearly seventy long years.

We are very old now. We cannot walk very well. Still, we think we would like to talk to this leader. We are the bombed people, and there are not so many of us alive anymore.

It is our job, we think, to speak for those who are not living.

We wish to say the things they could not say.

We get out of bed, and it is not easy, but we prepare to go to the appointed place. We get our hair fixed. We choose our clothes. We get the day service nurse to take us to the place where we are washed. We are washed like dishes, in a machine, or like underwear, by hand. We take the bus. We get our children to take us. Or else our grandchildren. Or a friend. Or we hire a taxi. Or we ask for a ride. There is so much to prepare. For days we are busy with preparing. Even on the bus. Even in the street. And it is not until we see the lines of police, the men in yellow clothes telling people to stay here, go there, that we know. The leader only has so much time. We cannot talk to the leader. The bombed people he will talk to were chosen, and they were chosen months ago. There are only two or three of them. They have been here for hours. What else did we expect? We were stupid to think it would be any different. Now the chosen ones are sitting on the other side of a metal fence from us and the crowd, and there are men in suits holding their elbows and telling them things.

We do not go into the crowd.

We are too old for that. We stay where we are, at the edge. At the back. After a while, from some other person's phone, we hear the voice of the leader and what he has to say. His voice is faint and we don't understand it. It is in a different language. After a little pause, there is another voice that speaks in the language we know. We nod along, trying to hear.

A person with a camera asks us if we are one of the bombed people.

Yes, we say. All the people in this city who are very old are bombed people. We can see us here and there in the crowd. We who were not chosen, but thought we might be. We who were bombed.

We are leaning on our children.

We are dizzy in the heat.

We say to the person with the camera: we are glad the leader has come to speak to us.

We are tired. We are not sad. We are tough as nails.

As a child, when the bomb fell, we buried our teachers. We buried our friends. On that day it was just as hot as this.

Nishina Sekio in a Broken Machine

He steers himself to the bottom of the sea. He is dying, so he cannot feel the pressure building in his ears, the ocean bending the membranes of his body, forcing its way into the machinery of his stomach and blood. Behind him the USS *Mississinewa* is breaking apart, swirling down like an ink blot, and from time to time Nishina notices the sun flitting in and out of cover above him, pieces of plunging steel trailing streamers of ash, fingers of oil, swimming toward the bottom as if reaching for some lost item, a promised gift.

Beyond the horizon of his mangled body, Nishina can see the white of the sand rising up to meet him from what looks like a thousand miles below, or maybe a thousand inches, the water making it impossible to tell distance, nothing available to judge by except a few darting shapes that might be fish or trash flitting around the impact of each piece of wreckage cratering the bottom. There is death all around him, Nishina still at the controls, knuckles bloodless around the rudder, the throttle, the blunt end of the folded periscope lodged in his skull, the sun arrowing through everything around him like a cathedral, a hall of golden columns candling in and out. In his mind, or what is left of it, Nishina is reaching for life, the last dregs of it feathering through his nerves, spasming in what remains of his spine. Like all bodies, his gathers speed, becomes heavier with depth, and still his hands keep hold of the levers, gentling his fall at a shallow angle toward the soft landing he can sense beyond the rim of his sight.

The darkness of the hallway at home: his first time back in years, when he opens the sliding door and there is nothing to greet him except emptiness, the polished grain of the floorboards reaching forever into the house, a blue vase of dead lilies just slightly off center in the alcove where his parents' shoes kiss neatly together at the heels and toes. His father is out, as he always is, but Nishina can sense his mother's presence on the far side of the wall, even before she calls out in surprise, wanting to know who it is in her hallway, a shadow approaching the frosted glass of the living room door. Late evening, and the sun is streaming into the house from his back, casting the outlines of soft branches onto his neck, his rounded shoulders, the divots behind his knees.

If she knows, she does not show it when she catches sight of his face. An unscheduled shore leave, just enough time to spend the night, and he knows his time is up, the decision already made. The frame of the old house is too low for a man of his height, and so this is how his mother sees him the first time, his last visit, his head bent to clear the doorway, his bright eyes tilted forward, almost seeming to look up at her, a slight woman with her bones pushing up through her skin, reaching with her arms to lift herself above the cabinet by her head.

There are a thousand things she wants to ask and not ask of him and they crowd her face like delicate fishes in the instant before she opens her mouth and nothing comes out. What Nishina had wished was to be the parent in this moment, to know what to do, but he finds himself a child, arms stiff at his sides, his body another's, lost to his thoughts.

Some moments never end, even as time goes on. His mother looking away, turning up the heat on the stove. The cheerful gossip over dinner, his mother not reaching for anything, claiming she has already eaten. Her grip on his arm when she walks him to the door the next morning, the way she keeps casting her eyes down the street, telling him to wait, saying his father might be back at any moment. The long walk down the block after they say their goodbyes, Nishina waiting to hear the rattle of the front door closing and never hearing it, not even when he turns the corner, not even when two boys on the street stop to salute his lapels and cap, something about their fingers too crisp, their backs too straight, as he leaves them too behind, the sun in his eyes.

Nishina Sekio at the controls of a broken machine, the sea in his mouth, his body unmoving, and in the doorway of the living room, his childhood before him, dappled in shadow, frozen in place.

Harvest Mouse

Her husband is dying, but still she goes to the mountains. She is saving the world, she says, though of course she is not. At best she is saving the western alpine harvest mouse. At worst she is wasting her time. She wants to be able to look future generations in the eye, she says, and say she did her part. From his bed, with his tattered veins, her husband says, that's right. Either you're part of the solution, or else you're precipitate. The old joke is still good for a good old laugh.

Her husband laughs with his eyes closed. He doesn't watch her start to leave. She only reaches for her jacket when he closes his eyes.

She goes to the mountains. She goes for weeks at a time. She gets her mother's texts in batches, at sea level, like spring rain. They explain, with plenty of redundancy, what she already knows: that her husband is dying just this once.

Her mother is wrong, though, about the other thing. It's really true. By the time her husband is in the ground, it is entirely possible that the western alpine harvest mouse will be out of time.

She goes to the hospital. She makes sure her husband is looked after. She tells him what she saw. A bird in the distance. A spider in her shoe. They laugh together, and she is gone again. Another week. Another absence.

Her in-laws put it to her in the bluntest way, because this is what in-laws do. Her husband's father says, it's only a mouse. You are abandoning my son for the sake of a mouse.

This is in the summer in the depths of a drought. A world of ants crawls in through the windows of her kitchen, seeking moisture. On the phone, with the radio turned low, she watches the little red bodies trekking across fields of newspapers, orange skins, coffee stains.

When she thinks of an answer, it is already Wednesday. She has washed her boots. She has stocked up on food. Ready to go. She thinks that to tell her it is only a mouse is like telling a pole-vaulter it is only the Olympics. I am a field biologist, she thinks. This is my world.

She doesn't tell this to anyone. On Thursday, she leaves.

It is an eight-hour drive to the mountains, and she drives alone. This is fine. She has spare drive belts in her trunk and a satellite phone in her glove compartment that costs a hundred bucks a minute, or just about, for emergencies. She has day markers in the back seat and flares under the dash, though the flares are long expired and it is possible that she is prepared for a breakdown during the day but not at night. The mountains come into view on the third hour like purple fog, and they turn steadily browner on approach. Her right hand skips through radio stations until she is left with the one where the ads run five minutes each. On either side of the highway, turning black against the sun, she passes signs that say *Pray for rain.*

The cabin looks out over a valley of grass and rock. In a few months, bright flowers with names like shooting star and Shasta daisy and snow-in-summer will color the view. She thinks of a tufted grass she has named Mary's misery because the sticky sap gets all over her boots.

For now there are the white flags marking the entrance to every nest. There is a hawk riding up the cliffs to her right. There is a cloud in the distance that reminds her of rain, though at this time of year she knows better. She carries in a ten-gallon jug of water from the car, and then groceries.

It is possible that the drought is what she is fighting against. The state wants to build a reservoir in this valley, and it would flood the mice out. So water and her husband are both things she is losing to this fight.

Before falling asleep she wishes she knew a way to describe the western alpine harvest mouse in a way that didn't involve the length of one of its toes or the precise dimensions of one of its teeth.

She wakes. She works. She loses track of time. The day her supplies run out, she drives back down the mountain into a world of clouds.

They sneak up behind her. They chase her down the road. By the time she makes it to the hospital there is weather all over the radio. The oldies station she has picked for the last few miles pulls its advertisements off the air. There is talk of a storm.

You made it, her husband says.

I'm here, she tells him.

Tell me about the birds, her husband says.

She tells him. And then she talks of other things, and he asks more questions. They exchange sentences the two of them will soon forget. From time to time someone comments on the changing color of the sky.

They leave the window open so as to be the first to know.

What happens is this: the rains never come. She watches the night lift. Sometime the next day, she loses her husband and then, not much later, her world.

Hack Science

The Bodega Bay Marine Lab is dedicated to the fish. I suppose this is kind of like dedicating a pig farm to the pigs. The whole place is packed full of ghosts, like sardines in a tin.

In another lab, in Virginia, I once came across a sign that said "Salt Is Our Enemy." You never know what people will fight for, or against.

That summer we kept sand sharks in a tank and thought up the best names, to make them famous. We thought a Hollywood reference might endear them to the press, so our sharks became Elsa, Mufasa, and the Hulk. Elsa kept dying from something in the water, so we had to name them Elsa II, Elsa III, etcetera.

The one reporter who finally arrived was from the University of Virginia. I think he promised us a story in one of their brochures. He wore a very official badge and ten-pound boots so we knew he was a stickler for rules. Asked if we had named the sharks, we told him that as scientists it was important to maintain our objectivity. We said their names were J1 to J10 if they were caught in July, and A1 to A6 if caught in August.

It turns out the best science is hack science.

Some other hack science I learned: the inside of a shark is a Monet painting. You can see water lilies or bridges or whatever you want in the indigo and fuchsia of the liver, the apricot and marigold of the stomach, the aquamarine of the bile.

Also, a shark heart will beat for hours after death. In a plastic tub of water it makes a graceful, hypnotic swimmer.

I suppose, someone said, a human heart would spin in circles. Mammals have too many chambers, we decided.

We didn't test this on the kind old man who had a heart attack in September while pulling in a dusky shark. He was strapped into the chair so we couldn't tell till it was too late. We thought he was just running out of steam, the rod tip slipping, the engine churning, the line screaming off the reel. What we did, because there was nothing else, was examine the shark. On the way back to port, when we cut through the body wall, we found it was a mother. The pups were too young, and we knew this, but even so we lowered them into the water like we thought something, at least, could be saved.

A Shark Is an Animal That Blushes When You Touch Its Face

ONE

From time to time she asks me how it was, and I tell her:

Some nights we watched squalls like pale lanterns drifting out to sea. Some mornings we saw the roads wriggle with rain and eels. Some days the turtles bubbled in their shells and we kept cool by crouching in the water in the tanks.

Shark tanks? she asks.

Yes, I tell her. But it wasn't any good. Even the sharks were panting from the heat.

It's always late at night when she asks such things. She tells me she just needs to hear another voice. She tells me: some places in the city, the trains only run at night.

Some fears are the same way.

TWO

The things that keep her awake. When they circle, and she holds them off, and there is nothing I can do to help the holding, she asks me. Something about sharks, she says, that focuses the brain. She says I could make up a reason for it, something involving words like fight-or-flight, but I won't.

I tell her a degree in marine biology has never felt so useful.

Look at me, she laughs. Trying to hold my shit together with my bare hands and still I find time to soothe your ego.

My ego is grateful as ever.

Don't let it get to your head, though.

Ask, my child, and you shall receive the wisdom you seek.

THREE

Let's be clear: laughter, not sharks, is the best thing.

FOUR

But some nights she will not laugh. So I tell her:

Until a shark decides to bite, you can never see the upper teeth. Only the lower teeth—narrow, needle-like, designed for holding and not cutting. The upper teeth lie flat against the roof of the mouth and even if you flipped the shark upside down and pried the jaws open you would still have trouble finding them.

What do they look like? she wants to know.

Smooth and opaque, but only in the center. Like something made from white caramel.

And feel?

Very sharp. The first thing you notice is the warmth of blood on your skin.

FIVE

What she wants, she says, is to tame her dreams. This is something she tries very hard, each night, to do. Every morning, in her journal, she checks her progress. Sometimes it takes an hour to account for every dream.

Why? I want to know.

She puts her hands to her eyes and speaks into her open palms: to know what I put myself through.

SIX

What I know is very little:

If she passes by a clinic, she will not go to sleep.

If she hears a certain song on the radio, she will not go to sleep.

If she is reminded of her father, she will not go to sleep.

When she dreams about sharks, she dreams them with all-black eyes.

SEVEN

Is that real? she wants to know.

Every eye is black in the center.

But the rest?

Gold, green, tan, blue in flecks or in a solid stripe. From up close the edges of the irises are ruffled like a wet book after it dries.

EIGHT

Conversation on a lazy Sunday morning:

Sleep well?

Like a log.

Woke up in the woodshed?

In a chimney, broken into a million gray flakes.

I wanted that to be a joke, I say, and suddenly, it is. We laugh so hard she ends up in my arms.

Try me again, she says, gazing up at me.

How do you make a shark float?

Don't know.

Use ice cream, root beer, and a shark.

When she smiles, the edges of her eyes film with color, like gasoline.

NINE

A different day, three a.m. A single set of footsteps ringing outside the dark windows and far away, the passing of a train.

She says she can't do it. She just can't. While saying this she holds her ears as if it is the sounds that are trying to force her. She says when you fall asleep you lose the last bit of you that disbelieves. Each time you wake up, it's so hard to know what wasn't real.

What do I do at a time like this? When they circle her like black limousines, when she holds them off and I can't help the holding?

I let her soothe my ego because it's all there is left.

I tell her a shark has a hide like a rhino's that bruises like the thinnest skin. When frightened they go pale. When touched on the snout, the pads of your fingers leave patterns like swirling rain.

I hold her hands.

Synonyms for Climate Change

There was Tabitha, who had to go home to look after her mother, who was dying soon, but not for four more years.

There was Arnav, who everyone said would be graduating early, until he was suddenly gone, on medical leave in Idaho or somewhere, until his visa ran out and nobody could get in touch.

There was Hector, who hit it big in his last year with a paper in the *Proceedings of the National Academy of Sciences* (pee-nas, he insisted on calling it to anyone who asked, long after it stopped being funny), and got a bear hug from the department chair at graduation and a tenure-track job without even trying.

There was Sarah, who could not wake up in time for classes or exams, not for anything, not even with two alarms and sometimes even after she asked friends to stop by her apartment, the key under a rock, and I would see her some mornings with her eyes open in bed, looking up, until it was depression and she was in therapy and then on drugs that also made her sleep and sleep.

There was Lulu, who only wanted a job in the Philippines and got it, a professorship in the city where her parents still lived, waiting for her proudly, with a job title and funding the likes of which we couldn't believe.

There was Troy, who pissed off his advisor somehow and finished up a coursework-only master's and joined the Coast Guard.

There was Toshiko, who graduated all right, but two years late, and found a job in DC that was good enough for now, she said, until she stopped writing in the fall and even her phone number wouldn't connect when we called her after that.

There was Kerri, who took a leave of absence to have a baby with Tada, who followed her home to Wisconsin. These were my two closest friends. On Skype, from across the country, we talked about being in with a chance of beating the odds. Tada was working on his thesis remotely, calling his advisor every week. Kerri was thinking about starting over somewhere else, maybe when she could sleep through the night again, when her head wasn't so foggy. Their baby, Emi, was a fat bundle of cotton and limbs on the screen that knew a few words that were words and many that weren't. Tada wanted his baby to hear Japanese being spoken around her so we talked about the weather or the news or all the friends we knew in grad school who had drifted out of our lives. There were so many of them, which shocked us, even now. We hadn't known when we started that the dropout rate would be half or that most of the other half would need six years to graduate, and we joked about the lowered bar, how success was a cakewalk now, was not being too ashamed to call back if someone called, was only being moderately depressed about what had happened with all the time we'd thought we'd had. We said persistence is the key to subsistence. We said gratitude is the best attitude. We said research jobs are a pyramid scheme, are a morbid business, year after year waiting for new openings, which was a euphemism for professors aging out of the workforce, which was a euphemism for death, and we lied a little or a lot when we asked each other if things were going all right.

In my fifth year, in 2010, they came back to campus. Tada to defend his thesis, and Kerri to cheer him on, she said, though we all knew that was not the only reason. They fought about this among themselves and on phone calls with me and on Skype with the three of us together, until they arrived on a Monday afternoon with a dozen suitcases and Emi in a baby carrier with flower-patterned straps. This was in the spring and the trade winds were blowing strong and constant. I kept a go bag that was a backpack with a water bottle and miscellaneous tools by the door to be ready to head to sea at any moment, whenever the winds dipped even a little and the swells were manageable. My advisor would pick me up at my apartment after ten and drive me down to the harbor. We were out all night and into the morning. We worked wordlessly and took breaks to throw up quietly over the rail. Starting before dawn, we would pull up deep-sea sharks. If dead on the line, their pale stomachs showed first in black water, like distant heat lighting. If alive, they were dark clouds with lanterns for eyes. They were soft and slow but stronger than you could imagine. When we tagged and released them, pulling fishhooks from jawbones with snub-nosed pliers and pushing them down, I thought this must be exhaustion, the way it plunged out of sight.

I smelled like diesel and fish blood when I hugged them at the airport. I was in my t-shirt and boardshorts, hair stiffened with salt. Kerri wore a summer dress over black tights and Tada a blazer and a crew neck, like he was Ozaki Yutaka or Magnum PI. They were whisper-fighting when I pulled up at the curb. Emi was asleep on Tada's back. There was drool in his hair. We hugged, and they laughed, and the fighting stopped.

Kerri was thinking of finishing her degree. Her plan was a master's, which she could get in a semester or two of classes, and then starting over on a doctorate somewhere else. She was going to meet with a professor who she liked and who she hoped liked her enough to help. This professor's name was Anita and she was sympathetic to Kerri because of what had happened last time. She had called Kerri once in Wisconsin, to check up on her, she said. She had said, if you want to cry, you should.

What had happened last time was a secret except to ten people. These were me and Tada, Kerri's advisor, the advisor's lawyer, a liaison officer, and five professors who served on a certain committee.

It terrified Tada to be back here with Kerri where they might meet these people in hallways, where they might see the secret on their faces and be expected, or not expected, to react.

Look at you, Tada said to me in the car. You look like Baywatch, he said, but you smell like a shithouse.

He smells like *data*, Kerri said from the back seat. Not like you and your computers, she said. Tada was a modeler, which Kerri and I said amounted to profiting off the hard work of data-collectors. Tada was amenable to this view, except when he would rub it in our faces by calling us the muscle and himself the brains.

I'll open the windows, I said. We were on the highway now and the ocean was a blue plate between the city and the sky.

God, Kerri said, I've dreamed of this.

What? I said.

Getting the fuck out of Sheboygan, she said.

Even Tada laughed at this, which woke up Emi with her round, astonished-looking eyes. Her first time seeing the ocean. She must have smelled it in the wind.

During the worst of it, Tada would call me from Wisconsin, scared out of his wits. Kerri gone, the car missing, in the middle of the night. He whispered the terrible things she had said in the days before. He sat hunched on the rim of the bathtub. Emi was in the bassinet on the far side of the door. He didn't know who to call. Kerri's parents couldn't know. This was the unspoken rule.

People change with distance. Or maybe what changes is the nature of a friendship without touch. When he was still on campus I used to go over to his apartment on days when Kerri was staying over and feel groundedness seep into me. He had cups and bowls but not a single glass. We drank cider, when we drank it, out of mugs, with ice. There was a framed picture of his parents holding him as a baby next to the bathroom door. Some evenings he played Asakawa Maki live and beaten-down and unafraid in 1977 in an auditorium in Kyoto on his CD player and I thought I knew why they were together, Kerri and him.

I met Kerri's advisor twice in the hallways. This was before he went to Sweden, first on sabbatical, and then permanently, the director of some institute they created just for him. Before then I had heard him on the radio. He was saving the world, he'd said, him and his brilliant, intrepid students. He himself was on a working group for the latest IPCC assessment report. He'd had a student write a draft of his section because, just because, he trusted them that much.

He was shorter than I'd assumed and thinner than I'd guessed from his voice. He did not look worried, or guilty. I could have said something (what?), but was not supposed to know.

There was Marco, whose advisor ran out of funding and was given the choice of paying his own way or leaving with nothing.

There was Grace, who was offered the chance to finish her degree in Belgium, and didn't take it.

There was EJ, who developed schizoaffective disorder, or who'd had it for years without knowing, without knowing, without knowing, until.

There was Frances, who became a lab manager, which paid her bills and let her do a little research on the side, from time to time, and who learned to eat lunch behind the agriculture building in September and October, to get a break from the new, ambitious students and their sympathetic eyes.

There was Leda, who became a government scientist, which was acceptable, she said, sounding truly happy on the phone from California, the wind in her hair.

I do not believe I am changing the world but I believe I am in with a chance of finding out how the world will change. There is a place of low oxygen concentrations, around six hundred meters down from where we are setting our lines. The sharks we tag move in and out of it, looking for food, and we want to know how this will change in the future, when the low-oxygen zones will only get bigger. This is a shark that lives in most of the oceans, from Alaska to Madagascar, from Iceland to Patagonia. If it turns out that they avoid certain oxygen levels, or can spend less time there, it would be like knowing that earthworms will be pushed out of certain types of soils. Things would become just a little different, in little pockets, everywhere at once.

The problem is funding. In September, after Tada has graduated, after they have moved to Norfolk for his new job—a postdoc—my advisor and I run out of money to buy new tags, to run the lab boat, everything. Two of the proposals we were counting on are rejected. We are looking for small money, anything that is quick and will keep us going. My advisor sends me texts in the middle of the night. Write me a draft for this funding call, it says, and then a link. The state research fund, conservation societies, fisheries councils, millionaire charities.

Anita does not agree to help Kerri get her degree. She has run out her leave of absence. She must start over, if she is to start over, if she can find a person who will hire her, a dropout.

I miss it, she says.

Miss what? I say.

Being a real person, she says.

She told me once, years ago, that right up until the moment it all went to shit, she'd thought she'd found what she was meant to do.

It started early, in the spring of her first year of grad school, ten months into the program. It was June and she was already in the field, on a "cruise," we called it, a research trip, six days on a ship the size of an apartment building turned on its side, pulling jellied creatures out of deep-towed nets and examining them for ten hours a day. She was too excited to sleep, too anxious to sit, too seasick to work, until she learned to work with a bucket of sick at her feet for instant relief that did not require running onto the deck and casting around to find the leeward rail. She was doing real work, she thought, she was adding her little marks into the scientific record in that windowless wet lab hunched over a dissecting microscope trained on a whole world dragged up from deeper than light in the ocean (viperfish, arrow worms, barreleyes, bristlemouths, snipe eels silvered and mangled and fantastical in metal dissecting trays and petri dishes and sample jars and loose Tupperware containers on the bench and all around her on the floor), she was finding her sea legs, she was blasting Rachmaninov into her earbuds to ward off the nausea, and she was standing at the rail after dinner and a shower, feeling the wind in her fingers, looking up at the city of the ship, the huge arc of the crane, the spinning antennae, and her advisor in his work vest, putting a palm on the wrong part of her shirt and asking if there was somewhere they could go. The sea was at her back. Her boots were unlaced and heavy on her ankles. She could hear people talking. She thought this couldn't be happening. It did, and it did.

She made an appointment with the liaison, who was listed on the university website. The liaison was not a mandatory reporter. She advised against going to the police or talking to anyone outside the department. Much later, Kerri said, she realized this liaison was not on her side.

In October, Kerri is gone for days. Norfolk is a small city and there is nowhere she would go, no one she knows, but still. Tada with Emi in her high chair, feeding her blueberries, his phone in the crook of his shoulder. He has called in sick for an important meeting. Emi is hungry but running a low fever, strangely subdued.

I can't do this alone, he says. I can't.

I find this not as worrying as when he says the opposite: I can do this alone, and I will.

A false alarm: Kerri calls from a motel near Ocean City, Maryland. She is coming home immediately, she says. She does not come home that night. She arrives the next morning.

I'm stuck, she says. I just needed to be somewhere.

Norfolk is somewhere, I say, but I think I know.

I am at home most days, finishing up a proposal for the fisheries council. They have read our pre-proposal, and they have gotten in touch. They like the direction of our research. We have tailored the language to their interests. We have emphasized that the sharks are in competition for prey with certain high-value fisheries species. We have said that in a climate-change future, there will be winners and losers, and there will be a premium in identifying the winners in advance.

They call my advisor. This is a private call, and they do not want to be on speakerphone. They have one suggestion. Maybe go easy on the "hot-button" terminology, they say. At their organization they are mindful of the controversy; they respect the views of every side.

Is this censorship? I say. I am in my advisor's office. The sun is setting through the window and the walls are awash in purple and branches. He looks tired, my advisor—he works hard, is on campus at seven in the morning and leaves after dark. He says: this is good news, they're trying to help us.

He rubs his jaw with his fingers in little circles, like he is feeling for a lump.

That's it? I say. We just take out that whole angle?

They suggested "extreme weather," he says. And maybe use something else. Make it seem natural.

Global environmental change, I say.

Exactly, he says.

And there it is: I've come up with something, I'm part of this now, I'm doing it.

The odd thing is that it's meaningless, this change. Anyone can tell that these are synonyms for climate change. And there are so many of them, I don't even have to repeat myself. Irreversible warming, climate regime shifts, temperature uncertainty, weather anomalies, increasing scope of variability, and on and on. Practically, there's no difference. It's still the same research. I run the find-and-replace function in Microsoft Word and nothing else changes.

Ocean deoxygenation, water-column stratification, surface-ocean acidification, long-tail risks, critical thresholds.

Large-scale perturbations. Climate-system hysteresis. Runaway warming. Ecological cascades. Extreme-temperature scenarios.

Just call it something else, the liaison had said. You want to use the right word. We need to be careful. Assault has a very specific meaning.

In November, Kerri calls with good news. There is a professor in Richmond who is thinking of taking her on. She has told him her secret, in confidence, and he understands. It's partly a matter of money now, and partly about fit. For one thing he doesn't know if she's really going to be able to handle the work and childcare and the commute from Norfolk on top of everything else. He wants her to come down to his office. Maybe he will give her a project that she can work on during the winter, as a volunteer, just to see how it goes. Even then she will be starting from nothing. She will have to take all the required courses. The professor thinks he can get funding to pay her stipend for four years, but he can't guarantee it. This is the best he can offer.

This is a good thing, Kerri says. I can feel it. I'm so relieved, I can't think.

Tada takes the phone. She's dancing with Emi, he says. Then I hear them dancing: heavy footsteps, Emi babbling, Kerri chanting Mommy's got a job, got a job, got a job.

A *volunteer* job, Tada says.

Mommy's gonna be a scientist, Kerri says.

Put me on Skype, I say.

On Skype we all do the dance together. We raise the roof with our hands and hop from foot to foot. It's not a dance, really, it's what your grandmother might do as a pantomime of young people dancing. Tada, the grounded one, doesn't even hop. He just stands back, does the hands, laughing and laughing.

In January, I get the money. It's not enough, but it's something. Enough to keep going for a little while at least. I might graduate in a year if things go to plan. I need a few more tags, enough clean data. I have two chapters of a thesis and a bit of the third. There's not much longer to go, if nothing goes wrong.

On the phone we talk about chances, about old friends in grad school. There was Tabitha, we say. There was Arnav. What's happened to Hector? Nobody knows. And then there was Sarah and Lulu. There was Toshiko and Troy . . .

Kerri, too, is still in with a chance. Her new advisor, who is named Bruno, takes her on officially. He is young, still in his thirties, not long out of grad school. It's a small operation, but he has ideas, and he seems professional, will not even drink on university property. One of his other students says he has never seen Bruno so much as raise his voice.

Tada worries, as always, though his anxieties are different now. His postdoc appointment is for two years at most, and the problem is staying in Virginia until Kerri finishes her program. He could work at a NOAA office maybe, or find someone in Richmond who will hire him for a little while longer. The options are slim, but it's a problem for another time. He could find something in Japan, take Emi with him, have his parents help with childcare until Kerri can graduate. He could come find me, if I am still in science somehow, he could find a job wherever I am and I could be Emi's godparent, I could look after her when Tada cannot. Teamwork makes the dream work, is what we say. It's unlikely, but it could happen.

As for me, I am still working, and I do my best. The new tags arrive in February and they are beautiful—fat black slugs that fit in the palm of my hand, smelling like winter when we open the box. They arrive in the afternoon on a Tuesday, and on Wednesday I put to sea. It's a clear, brisk day. The swells are rough but manageable. My advisor applies high-SPF sunblock to his nose until it looks carved out of chalk or soapstone on the brown of his face. Our longlines, which have been soaking for months in rainwater, smell like mud, feel like eels when we run them through our hands. All morning we work off the stern of a yacht that I think says *Fraud*, in blue cursive on white, until the tide changes and I see that it's *Esmeraude*, a name.

Boundless Deep

I don't remember why I was in the car. What I remember is that there was a tsunami warning. It was coming from Japan—this was the big one, off Fukushima—but it was a long way away, and we had time. A tsunami in open water moves about as fast as an airplane. This is something you could use to guess the arrival time even before running a wave model or pulling up buoy data from Saipan or the Azores. A direct flight takes ten hours, give or take, depending on the direction. So right off you could know that it would hit at night. In the meantime, the footage was coming in of what it had done to Kesennuma, Ishinomaki, Natori, Sendai. The odd thing was how easily the ocean can hide even the biggest wave. A tsunami is just inches tall in the open sea. The DART buoys were the only things that could get a reading on it. It took a few hours for those readings to come in, and even then, after Saipan, there was nothing. When it came to the final wave height, across all that dark water, it was hard to know for sure.

Back then I lived up a ridge in a house that was divided into four apartments. I shared part of the top floor with a grad school friend in the same department, and the bottom floor, which was really the basement, was divided between two families. The one who got the worst deal was the neighbor on our floor, who was also a student, but in business accounting or something. He rented out a single room with a closet for a shower and not even a stove to cook on. We hardly ever talked to the guy. We only heard him early each morning running a vacuum cleaner over his forty square feet of carpet for some reason we could never understand.

We complained about having to climb the hill, but on days like this it meant we were safe. We had friends in the inundation zone who had to clear out every time there was a warning. Once the sirens go off, the cell network gets to be like midnight on New Year's—you can't get through. It helped that Cam and Rosa worked near campus, so they could drop by our building to say when they were planning on coming over and what they could contribute from their fridge.

The other thing that happens is that every person with a boat in the water heads out to sea. If you're far enough out you can take whatever wave. Mark, my advisor, was the only one allowed to drive the lab boat, so he always had to get to Sand Island, where the boat was docked. Maybe he figured he could kill two birds if we also loaded up for a trip we were planning for next week, or maybe he just needed someone to cast off lines and take the truck back. We were tracking snappers that year, and part of the way we did it was by mooring signal receivers around the island. There were thirty or forty of these things, and each one was anchored by two thirty-pound slabs of concrete. Every few months, when we pulled up the receivers to download data and put in new batteries, we'd have to line up these blocks on the dock and load them onto the boat by hand.

It must have been some kind of work he wanted to get done. Mark was all about killing two birds. Sometimes he'd have us doing carpentry below deck while he steered the boat into port, the bow skipping and slamming over swells as we braced ourselves in a corner, trying not to let the drill slip. Or else we'd be up on the front deck before dawn, chopping up frozen fish to use for bait, one of us holding the slippery bullet-shaped bodies against the lid of a cooler while the other tore into them with an electric saw.

He sent me a text, but by the time he pulled up outside the house I still hadn't gotten it. I heard his big Chevy climbing the hill and that's how I knew. There was a Y-intersection a couple houses past ours where he would always do a three-point turn. The clatter of his busted CV joints in the middle of that turn could wake me out of any kind of sleep.

Yasmine, my roommate, said: You don't owe him a thing.

The week before, Mark had told me how he was going to have to let me go. He'd been running out of money the whole year, and now it was down to me or Lisa. Yasmine had reacted the worst when I told her what happened.

I'd like to smack him in the face, she said. She'd also been friends with Sonoko, who'd left in the winter. Sonoko had gone on short notice, almost without saying goodbye, as though she were embarrassed to admit she was heading home. She'd had the option of staying on with a different advisor, but she'd have to pay her own way, and in the week before she left she still talked as if she might actually come up with the two thousand bucks she needed for the first payment. In the picture we took together outside the airport she looked like a tourist, wearing too many clothes and holding a yellow suitcase in one hand that contained everything she was taking with her.

It's probably nothing much, I said, when I went into my room. I didn't know what we'd be doing, but I was sure I needed board shorts and gloves. I took a bottle of water, because you never know, and a pocketknife, which Mark had drilled into us to carry at all times. A knife was a way of saving your life if you ever got snagged in a line or on a hook, he said. He nagged us all to buy one and he checked us individually to be sure we could flip the blade open one-handed, and with gloves on. Mark was like that. In some ways he looked after you like this was all that mattered.

Tell him to stop fucking over my friends, Yasmine said, when I pulled on my sneakers. She said it loud enough that Mark could probably hear. But he just sat in his truck, one arm out the window, listening to the radio on low. The announcer was saying the wave was expected in the early hours. He said it might not look like much at first, but a tsunami wasn't like a normal wave, it packed more punch.

By this time nobody needed to be told that kind of thing. At first I'd tried calling the few friends I still had in Tokyo, but I couldn't get through. The early reports were that everything was fine, the buildings had safely ridden out the quake, but a little later, news started trickling out about what had happened further up the coast. I can't remember if that picture of the ferry perched high and dry atop a building came out that day, but there was enough news in any case to know that something terrible and unimaginable had happened.

It was a warm night, with a little breeze that made the leaves of the papaya trees clap in the neighbor's yard. The moon was out, and a few patches of pale clouds drifted down off the mountains and out to sea. The long, trailing wail of the civil defense sirens, starting low, moving high, and then fading low again, seemed to come from everywhere at once.

This won't take long, Mark said, when I climbed into the car.

It doesn't matter, I said, throwing my bag in the back seat. The back of Mark's truck was always full of gear and junk. Fishing poles, tackle boxes, cases of beer, and those big gray Hefty buckets we used for storing cables and line. At night it was impossible to tell it all apart.

The man on the radio was saying the wave could be three to six feet high, or it could be well over ten, depending. It depended on the specific topography of the seabed, he said, sounding as though he was reading the words from a book. Toe-PAH-graph-ee, he said, enunciating every syllable.

You know, Mark said, I've never been inside your apartment. He said this as he turned the wheel, hand over hand, like steering a ship. His hands were marked by a dozen fresh and healing cuts, which he only ever treated with super glue. He would pinch the sides of the cut together and hold it like that until his fingers stuck and he'd have trouble tearing them apart. The glue would cure into white lace sheets that flaked away over the next few weeks. In the light of the dashboard they looked like slug trails, swarming all over his skin.

You should have me over, he said, turning to me.

Sure, I said, sliding my seat backward, trying to get comfortable. I reached down into the footwell and found a can of old fishing weights and a three-pack of flares, which I tossed behind me, starting off a miniature landslide when they crashed atop the pile of things and slid toward the floor.

The eerie thing about a tsunami is how hard it is to believe in, even when you know it's coming. It's not like a storm, which you can see and smell and feel the dampness of it settling on the ground before it lands. I slept through the last tsunami, from the earthquake in Chile, which ended up being barely a few inches by the time it got to us. I stayed awake for the one before that, when I was still in high school, before I left Japan. I lived inland, but the school was right next to a shipping port. You could even see the high white cranes looming over our soccer field. At night, on the news, I watched the white numbers inside yellow boxes that showed the wave heights along the coast. Every half hour you could see the tsunami wrap a little further around the peninsula and nose into the bay. Of course what I was really wishing for was just enough destruction to cancel school for a little while. But the wave was only a foot or two, and the next morning, even standing by the hurricane fence separating the school from the harbor, you could barely tell anything had changed.

The night Mark drove me down to Sand Island, it wasn't that the roads to the ocean were empty, but that most of the cars we saw were headed the other way. There were no station wagons stuffed with all they could carry, no vans with box springs strapped to the roof. We passed a few trucks trailing fishing boats with blue bimini tops and rusted outboards. These were the people who had opted to pull their boats out of the water rather than fuel up and head out. From a distance, the tallest boats loomed into view like thunderclouds.

They seemed to drift in on their own, riding invisible waves that surged up the street.

Crazy night, Mark said.

I guess it is, I said.

It's always a pain in the ass, he said. All this running around. Gathering supplies.

His phone was in his lap and he kept checking it for texts. The background was a picture from some fishing trip, and each time he turned on the display the pale buckskin of the fish he was holding up to the camera bloomed across the stubble of his chin. It made him look gaunt, that color, the way it clashed with the green of the streetlights, dividing up the hollows of his jaw into two sets of highlights, two sets of shadow.

No offense, he said. I mean, I know you have people over there.

He drummed his fingers against the steering wheel. He whistled hoarsely through his teeth. This man, he could never be still, not for anything. When he called you into his office, he would circle his desk the long way around. He would walk you to the door and back. There was something manic about it, the quickness of his movements, the intensity with which he would scan your face as he talked.

I called her, I said.

Who?

Sonoko. Today.

Oh. He kept his eyes straight ahead, but it seemed forced, the way he tensed his shoulders, leaning over the wheel.

No one picked up, I said. She's probably fine.

But it rang?

Yeah, I lied.

It felt, all of a sudden, like I had pushed too deep. The truth was that Sonoko's number had been just as dead as all the others. It gave me a three-tone beep, and then a robotic woman telling me the call could not be connected. But the hurt rose to Mark's eyes immediately, like a fish to a fly. It had been easier to think he wouldn't care.

I don't even have her address, he said. Not even—

His phone lit up, and his eyes flicked down for a second. His thumb hovered over the message app, but he didn't open it.

Only the shittiest texts get through, he said.

What is it? I said.

Lisa, he said. Says don't count on her. She has some excuse.

He shook his head and looked at me with disgust.

You students, he said. You're like a clique. You never tell me the fucking truth.

He pulled off into a side street and spun the truck around. There was a rasping, metallic noise and I could feel some part of the driveshaft knocking under my feet. When we climbed onto the freeway, the ocean rose up in the distance behind the square blocks of the hotels and car dealerships. On the other side of those waves, I thought, parents were digging through rubble, searching for their children. This was impossible, but it was true.

The day Mark told me he was letting me go, he said if there was some deal with my visa, like with Sonoko, he was sorry, but there was nothing he could do. I told him it wasn't like that, but I was probably going back anyway. I couldn't think of any other fallback plan. Mark never gave us any notice, which was part of the problem. But still, I couldn't seem to make the call to my parents. I bought a plane ticket, told the landlord when I was moving out, and still. I packed up my office, checked out the books I was going to steal from the library, and still.

On Skype, I paused over Sonoko's name. Her icon was a picture of herself testing out a receiver just outside the harbor. The water was dark, almost pure black in the picture, but Sonoko's arms and hair were vivid with light. The sun moved in ribbons over her head, her wetsuit, and seemed to glow from inside her mask. There was a pale spot, which could have been a bubble, or maybe a jellyfish, at the right edge of the picture, not far from her leg.

It was early evening, which made it midmorning in Iwaki, but she picked up on the third ring. Her voice was hoarse, like she was coming off a cold, but she could have just been asleep. She must have recognized the jumble of digits that marks out a Skype call.

Yasmine? she said, before I could get a word out. Even among our grad school group, I was not her closest friend. Or maybe we had been the kind of friends whose closeness only made sense in certain contexts. Late evenings on the lab boat, sitting with our backs against the cabin to watch the onrushing waves, we'd had no need for words. We had little in common except the most important things.

How are you holding up? I said.

She sighed, and for an instant I was listening to the phone plunged into a wave, the current billowing past, dragging it along the bottom of a reef.

Good, she said finally. My dad's allergic to puppies, she said. I think I might have to give Momo away.

Damn, I said. That's awful. I'm busy right now, but I'm going to send you things, okay? Whatever you need.

I've got a job, she said. I work at a store now. It's not so bad, you know? she said. It's my secret power, being a fish expert. At the sushi place, if I get really wasted, I use the Latin names.

Look, I said. I have to go.

Here's a seagull, she said, and I heard her thrust the phone out, and the scrabbling of something small and desperate in the air. There was the rustle of the wind, and the whirring of the light, boxy cars I remembered from before I left. I kept listening for a bird to squawk, but I couldn't make it out.

Listen, I'm working out a life, she said, and hung up.

That night in Mark's car I kept thinking of that seagull, kept trying to play out in my mind how far that bird would have strayed from the Pacific to hover over Sonoko's head.

Mark slammed on the brakes just after we got off the freeway. We hadn't been going very fast, but still there was that moment of speed and sluggishness at once, like skidding on ice, when the outside world seems to drift in slow motion even as it pins you to your seat. I was staring at the flat bark of a tree we were heading toward, creeping up to the passenger side door, and I was thinking how it was probably an African tulip tree, based on the pattern of the bark, and that at least I knew the name of the thing that was going to crush me. Then we hit the curb with a softer bump than seemed possible and the truck came to a stop with one wheel canted onto the sidewalk. There was a long rasping sound, like the car exhaling. One of us must have hit the dial on the radio during the crash, and now it was crooning out Hank Williams, mid-chorus, singing about the banks of the old Pontchartrain.

I reached across and clicked it off. The silence, when it arrived, was overwhelming.

This was between downtown and the airport, where there were self-storage sheds and machining factories on one side and car rental places and food service companies on the other. The jail was a little way down the road. Because we were just off the water, everyone had long since cleared out. It was odd, after the whirling streetlights of the freeway, to see nothing but dark. You could always smell this section of road, even with the windows closed, which was like the smell of an empty dumpster after a hot day. The wind, or something, must have pushed one of the garbage bins over, and no one had been around to pick it up. The big black plastic bin was in the middle of the street, the lid flapped open, jars and paper and smashed-up food scattered across two lanes. From time to time the breeze picked up a plastic sheet and twirled it like a ghost in the beams of our headlights.

Jesus *fuck*, Mark said, breathing hard. His left foot was tapping against something, or maybe it was trembling.

Well, are you going to move that thing out of the way? he said.

It was cozy and cool inside the truck. I'd been half-asleep when we'd squealed to a stop. I didn't want to get out, but I elbowed the door open. A pocket-sized knife sharpener and a tube of green grease clattered out of the truck. I saw them hit the road and then bounce out of sight. I peered over the side of the footwell—it suddenly felt like a long way to climb.

I'm going, I said.

Get going, he said.

I picked up the bin and wheeled it onto the curb. The wheels kept coming up against hard pieces of trash and I had to push with my shoulder to make any progress. The plastic was warm and sticky against my palms. When I was done, I turned and saw Mark leaning over midway between me and the truck. When he stood up, his arms were full of mustard-stained paper and boxes and clear plastic food containers. He kept reaching down and picking up more things.

None of this is my fault, Mark said, when he passed me on the way to the bin.

I couldn't just have you do all the work, he said more gently when he came back, unburdened. There was a smear of something, maybe some kind of sauce, across the top of his cheek.

That's right, I said. You're right.

He used his shirt to wipe the smear from his face. This was a long-sleeved Lycra shirt that was already so stained with grease and fish that you could hardly tell the difference.

When we climbed back into the truck, Mark flicked on the radio and tuned back into the news. The announcer was saying that certain bays and inlets were likely to see a larger wave. He was saying there could be multiple waves; that it was best to stay away from the coast for a good long time. It was comforting, hearing that same careful voice, still saying all the same careful things. The waves could arrive in sets, he said. Each one could crest for ten or fifteen minutes, he said. The announcer had a deep, rasping voice. He droned on and on.

When Mark turned the key in the ignition, the car coughed and coughed, but it wouldn't start.

Yasmine was the one who first heard the talk about Mark. She was more outgoing, was in all sorts of clubs and committees, and she picked it up from a student who was visiting from a school in Georgia. Mark had been a professor there for a few years before he came to us. He didn't exactly have the best reputation when he left, this student had said.

Rosa came over for dinner the day Yasmine found out. On the veranda, sitting around a rotting office table, the three of us divided up a meatless lasagna into unequal pieces and played rock-paper-scissors for the right to pick the first piece.

Before Georgia, Yasmine told us, Mark had gotten his start up north, in Massachusetts. It was a big school, a hugely rich program, and there was a ton of pressure. Everything had looked great for Mark until the rumors started, in his fourth year, that he had made up some data. Not fudged, Yasmine said, but straight-up created. Part of the problem was that the data was something he'd been working on for years; he'd already used it to publish three papers. As scientists we're obligated to write just the facts, some collaborator had said, but if this is true, this man is writing a novel. There was an internal investigation and all sorts of proceedings, but in the middle of it all, just when it looked like the findings would go out to the public, Mark disappeared. He turned up in Georgia a few months later. This was a sleepy program with only a few faculty, and they must have been thrilled to see a résumé like his. The suspicion was that his old department had decided to put a lid on the whole thing by getting rid of him—that anything had seemed preferable to staining their reputation with fraud. That they'd even recommended him, said they were sorry to see him go, and this place in Georgia was too eager to believe it.

But this lasted for just a few years, Yasmine said. People talk, and eventually that talk got to Mark's bosses. One of them, supposedly, was an old friend of the chair. So Mark had left again, right in the middle of a semester. He was running all over the damned country, Yasmine said. If he had stayed in Massachusetts or Georgia he probably would have been banned from government funding. He would have been kept out of this line of work for life.

Rosa, who had a flair for drama, kept saying holy moley, over and over again. Yasmine, who was earnest and had a protective streak, kept asking what I was going to do. Whatever you decide, I'll help you, she said.

But I couldn't decide. By that point I was already three years into my degree. I was scared of getting set back all that time if I tried to find another advisor, if I would even be able to find one. I didn't know if Mark would poison the well by telling people I was a liar or a lousy student. I would be sunk then. You couldn't do anything without a solid recommendation. You couldn't survive without being vouched for by someone who had believed in you enough to pay your way. You couldn't get any kind of job without a degree, no matter how many years into it you were when you stopped.

Sonoko had said, I'm nearly done, I'll just wait it out. And then Mark had started running out of money, and then she was gone.

It was so dark on that road off the freeway. With the hood popped open, you couldn't see a thing inside. Mark used his phone, which only made the soot-covered engine glow a dark red. He had me sit in the cab and turn the ignition. Through the windshield I saw him kick the bumper and punch the hood.

There's that 76 past the intersection with the access road, I said. Maybe there'll be more light over there.

Mark lowered the hood and came over to the driver's side. His phone was still on, and this time I saw that it was a pollock contorted in front of Mark's chest, his scratched-up fingers lodged in its gills. That's an Atlantic fish, I thought. I wondered if it was a picture from Massachusetts, from the days when the future had still seemed impossible to constrain. He looked younger then, grinning behind the fish that had been purposefully thrust out toward the camera to make it seem bigger than it was. Mark was the one who had taught me this trick. A fisherman isn't under any obligation to tell the truth. I wondered if it had been a one-time thing, this lie he had told. I wondered if it was possible that he had been running all these years from one mistake.

I don't have any better ideas, Mark said.

He took the wheel and the door, and I pushed from the back. It helped that the road was perfectly flat. It was tough going at first, but once the truck started rolling, it was manageable. Except for the corrugated siding of the storage sheds on the left and the blank space of the overflow Budget lot on the right, there was nothing to see. The headlights, which were sputtering out, would cross the endless distance of the blacktop and flare against the green and white road signs that were forever ahead. We had time, we still had plenty of time, but here we were, on a road next to the ocean pushing a truck on its last legs, and somewhere out there, I thought, a wave was coming.

Not long after that picture was taken of Sonoko testing the receivers, I remembered, she had come close to dying. A box jelly, a pale little bag of water and deadly poison, had brushed the inside of her knee, and she'd gone into anaphylactic shock. Our first aid kit had a brand-new AED and an oxygen tank but not a single EpiPen. It had been a near thing: Sonoko drawn and pale in the cabin, wheezing into a bag valve mask. This was a few years ago, around when I'd first started in the lab. Sonoko had been the only other student back then, and she had been around for some time. She had deeply tanned hands and salt-bleached hair, and she looked out for me whenever she could. This was going to be the trip where she taught me some of the things she did so I could take over her job someday and she could concentrate on writing her thesis. We had gone out and set up ten receivers on that trip. It was backbreaking work, but we headed to port with a little daylight to spare. On the very last stretch, when we were still a safe distance out from the breakers that rolled in on either side of the entrance to the harbor, Mark had stopped the boat and said we might as well do one more thing.

Sonoko was supposed to jump into the water with the receiver. I would trail a transmitter on a line off the stern and Mark would slowly drive the boat forward until we had gone about a hundred yards. The idea was to test reception over distance. This wasn't the best way to do it, but it was what we could do in the moment. Only once we had gone about fifty yards, I heard a scream and looked up to see Sonoko in the water, flailing both her hands above her head.

A box jelly is almost impossible to see except in the best of conditions. You look for the little flush of whiteness at the base of the tentacles. You look for the tiny black grains of the eyes. Ten days after the full moon, they rise out of deep water and wash into shore. Chances are, where there's one, there's more.

I remembered these facts while Mark gunned the boat toward Sonoko, threw the engine into neutral, and raced down the ladder. When he ran onto the back deck, I was remembering how the sting marks form a frosted ladder pattern, which is a mass of red welts that look like if a snowflake grew into the shape of a city grid. The pain was unbearable, I had heard. A burning, electric pain. While I remembered this, Mark took a running leap off the transom and dove into the waves.

Watch out, Sonoko found the presence of mind to yell. Somehow she managed to grind out the sentence: I think it's still here, somewhere around my leg.

It was hard to know what to think. It was hard to think of that man who arrowed off the boat that day as the same person who held so much power over our lives. I thought of Sonoko in front of the airport with her yellow suitcase, her ridiculous hat, waving us off before we could even try to follow her through the door. I thought of her in Iwaki, holding out her phone, a small, hopeless seagull hovering over her head. I thought that a wave was coming, coming from where Sonoko lived. I didn't know if it had gotten her, if she was already gone, and now it was coming for us.

The ocean was dull and flat on our right. It lapped against the concrete shore break and made sucking noises over riprap. Under the long piers that stretched out to sea, white frothy crests flashed between pilings and raced their way to shore. Ahead of me, the truck was a big square of night, lurching like a ship, the suspension creaking like dock lines over each wheel. We crossed a long sweep of road around a block of warehouses, and then the flat roof of the 76 floated into view above a wash of light.

There was a dip in the asphalt about midway between us and it. And then a gentle rise that climbed until you reached the lot.

I felt it first in my feet, and then in the weight in my hands. We took a few steps, then a few more, and stopped.

I could get out of here. This is what I thought. I thought it, and realized I had been thinking it for a long time. I could walk into the main part of the city. I could catch a ride home. I could climb the hill to Yasmine, and to Cam and Rosa, who would be there already, waiting for me.

Hey, Mark said. Hey, are you pushing? he said.

Come on, he said. We can do this, he said.

I had the sudden crazy thought that Mark would be going on the run again, that he would take the boat out from Sand Island and drive it off into the boundless deep. I imagined canned food buried under the junk in the back seat. I thought of the knife sharpener, the fishing weights, the emergency flares. I pictured all the things he would need to take. It made me angry, thinking this. That it could just keep happening. That when I was gone, Mark would be in Guam, or Saipan, or Kiribati. That it would start all over without me, or Lisa, or Sonoko.

I could send a letter to the dean. I could send it to anyone. It would be easy, I thought. I had nothing to lose.

Mark must have been staring ahead, keeping the lights in his field of vision, because I could see the silver lines of tendons in his straining neck. I could see the smudge of his breath on the driver's side window, how the halo of it fluttered like a pulse.

Help me, Mark said.

He looked tired. His shoulders. His hands. He just looked tired.

Please, he said.

You don't have to do this, Sonoko had said to me once. This was when we were putting out receivers, when we had to lift the concrete anchors from the back deck down onto the swim step. Standing with my hands in a tangle of galvanized chain, waiting for the right trough between waves to scramble down the three-foot drop. She was teaching me to do what she did so she could work on her thesis full time. It was about her own convenience as much as anything. But it was also about all of us. A bad step could sandwich me against the rail with sixty pounds of concrete behind me. Or if the shackle we had rigged as a safety gave way, it could send me down. At any moment it could all go wrong. We were out there in wind advisories, in the pitch dark, in twelve-foot swells. In the worst weather we would see the beam of Mark's headlamp sweeping over us, Mark standing high up on the center console, tossed by waves, his face pale with sweat and nausea, watching over us to be sure that we never let our feet stray seaward of the chain.

Listen to me, Sonoko had said. You only have to do what you can.

I couldn't explain it. On a night like this, when nothing made sense, I couldn't understand it. How we had gone from owing each other our lives, to this.

I pushed.

I pushed with my legs, my back, my arms. I pushed with my head jammed up against the tailgate, my neck at a painful angle, my chin in the crook of my shoulder. My bones ached, and I pushed until they didn't.

Slowly at first, almost too slowly to notice, the truck began to shift. It moved with a screeching, churning noise, as if it too were straining, reaching for higher ground. Little by little, whorls of red and orange and white reached across the curves of the metal in front of my face. I could see the green of reflected fishtail palms, the muted pink of azaleas, the white line that we crossed as we crested the hill and turned off the road.

When Mark reached the first gas pump, the steep angle of the light broke the flat of his back into a million pieces. His shirt had ridden up over his torso and I could see the soft skin of his waist. He didn't close the door immediately, or walk out to the front of the truck. He slumped against the driver's seat, his head in the footwell.

I knelt on the road with my hands on the bumper. My mouth was dry but there was sweat beading on the end of my nose, falling into a dark patch on the ground.

This was it. This was what I could do.

Either the truck would be fixable or I would find another way back. Either Mark would take the boat out of the harbor or he would head for safety with me. Back at my apartment, coming in from the night, I would find Cam and Rosa on the floor, stretched out on the carpet, surrounding some kind of board game that Yasmine would be winning. There would be watermelon slices in little square dishes, and Cam would have brought some kind of beer. When I opened the door, there would be quiet music playing. Rosa would have her head in the crook of Cam's elbow. She would say holy moley when I told the story of how we almost crashed the truck.

During Mark's night on the water, the wave would pass under him, and he wouldn't even notice. In the morning he would nose under the blinking shipping cranes of the empty harbor, the salt-gleamed concrete of the bridge, and pull into the slip. Everything would be the same, or nothing would. The streets would be impassible, or they would not. I would wake to the cool of the land breeze stalling against my window. I would know that I couldn't call Japan until early afternoon. I would make up a little box of things to sell, and things to give away. I would clean up the house. I would put together lunch for the two of us, or four of us, depending. I would sit around the rotting office table on our veranda and play rock-paper-scissors. Then I would open up Skype, scan down the list of names, and click.

This is what I could do. While Mark tinkered with the engine, I stayed bent over in the dark, my eyes on nothing, catching my breath.

My Grandmother Stops Some Nights on Her Way to the Outhouse to Watch a Ghost Climb Down to the Sea

The story goes like this: Izanami is a goddess who births the world. Her husband is Izanagi. They meet on a bridge in the sky and fall in love. Her first pregnancy is difficult, and she births only broken things that collapse into bubbles. After that, her body gets the hang of it and she births whole islands. She births gods and goddesses of the stones and trees. Of the earth and sea. At the end, she births a god of fire and it burns her alive.

The husband, Izanagi, tries to retrieve her from the land of the dead but she doesn't want to go. She is angered by his rescue attempts, so much that she grows to want to hurt him. She sends her monsters after him. She sends a whole army of killers. In death she has become even more powerful than when she was alive. Izanagi runs for his life, and he is barely fast enough. The last thing he does before he escapes the land of the dead is haul a boulder across the threshold so that nothing, not Izanami's monsters nor anything fierce and good that might someday want to rejoin the living, can ever follow him out.

Thousands of years pass. The people multiply in the land of the living and pass in time into the land of the dead and the gods fade into myths and legends. There are fires and famines and many wars big and small that are named and forgotten, until a war begins that is so vast and destructive that it is named after the world. My grandmother, fleeing that war in Osaka, settles down in a town in the mountains a short walk from the place where Izanagi is said to have emerged from the land of the dead. It's a small town, far from any bombs or fighting, and here my grandmother meets my grandfather and gradually, begrudgingly, she falls in love.

Her mother-in-law, on their wedding day, reminds her of the story. It's a famous story, one that everybody knows, but still. Izanami birthed a world of life but ended up god of only the dead. Things weigh heavier on some of us, the mother-in-law says, touching a hand to my grandmother's shoulder. The war is over now, and yet my grandmother's father, who stayed behind in Osaka, has been missing for years. The mother-in-law has watched the slow dimming of hope in my grandmother's eyes, and she has heard my grandmother's footsteps wandering the town on quiet nights, when she can't sleep.

And my grandmother remembers this—the story. She remembers it when her first pregnancy ends in miscarriage after four months. She remembers it when her second pregnancy ends, after long and punishing labor, in stillbirth. She remembers it when, six years after the war, long after the end of any expectation of life, she receives a letter from a man who says he recognized her father burned and dead by a road near the end of the war and her grief is sudden and madness-making. She remembers it that autumn, still frantic with loss, when she learns she is pregnant a third time and feels sick, not with pain or nausea, but with the conviction that her body is a path with no exit. A tunnel that has been blocked off with heavy stones.

Her husband, her in-laws, say her body will get the hang of it. Her mother says her body will get the hang of it. Sometimes it takes a few tries for everything to be ready. But most nights my grandmother vomits the acid and bitterness of her stomach into a bowl by her bed and then the fear and anger that heave out in sticky strings and then nothing but air and spasms in her diaphragm until she can carry the bowl outside through the kitchen door and across the open ground to the outhouse. The outhouse is damp and sour with hay and shit and the night air is a shock to her skin but clean, and one night in October she pauses on her way to the outhouse and sees a ghost stepping lightly on the road that leads down from the mountain and she remembers it again—the story, the goddess. How she remained with the dead. And instinctively, nonsensically, she believes that this small and lavender body that shines against the dark of the trees is that goddess. The goddess Izanami, escaped from the land of the dead, walking to the sea.

In the story, the goddess turns hideous, is rotted by death, but the ghost that walks down the road is neither ugly nor beautiful. She is short, big-boned, with an archer's long forearms sticking out well past the sleeves of a loose-fitting robe. There is nothing about the ghost that should make my grandmother think of the stories she has heard. But still, she believes.

She thinks of telling her husband, her mother-in-law, but doesn't. This is her own private magic. It is too delicate to share. It's not that anyone would doubt her—her in-laws are deeply spiritual, if not exactly religious, and she is certain that they would never accuse her of lying—but the next night, as she again stands on the path to the outhouse with a bowl of her pain in her hands, as she again watches the strange woman like a star dazzling the hills, she begins to feel that she alone is meant to see this. That someone, somewhere, has intended it for her.

Her days are short and full of labor. Winter is approaching, and there is no time to waste. There is wood to stack, kerosene to haul into the storeroom, rice to separate from stems and to hull, vegetables to harvest or swaddle against frost and snow. Well-water is cold now, and it blisters her hands. Her stomach is full. She squats in grass or bushes to pee because it's too far to the outhouse, and the urge too quick.

Her mother-in-law dies in April, of pneumonia, a long progressive disease that she hides until the very end, wheezing in the privacy of a hallway or in the dark of her room, and in May, as though in exchange, my grandmother gives birth to a daughter. There is no time to grieve. The child is alive and a fighter but underweight and feverish, born with skin more gray than red, and most of her first three years of life are spent going back and forth to the hospital in the nearest city. The doctors cannot say what is wrong with her, although they know that a simple infection or cold should not affect her this much, or for so long. There are tests of a dozen kinds that are each painful and inconclusive and cost more than my grand-parents can afford. The money they borrow, first from relatives of my grandfather's, and then from friends and neighbors and even the friends of their neighbors, anyone they can find. The pain my grandmother learns to look away from—the tangled red bruising on her baby's arms and the nurse apologizing about another collapsed vein and the exhaustion on the child's face each time they leave the hospital, the sleep that closes over her on the long trip by motorcycle back up the mountain roads, until one day my grandmother calls an end to the testing and the doctors and still the child survives.

My mother grows up a quiet child doted on by adults whose kindness she takes for granted. She spends her days climbing the persimmon trees in my grandparents' orchard, or catching tadpoles in puddles, until she is ready to hike the two miles through the woods with other children from the town to reach the nearest school. She is seven and then eight and she doesn't know why her parents work so hard each day but are always in debt, why even after their neighbors in the town are finished in the orchards her parents do hired work in rice paddies in the valley or in cucumber fields by the river, but she is not unhappy, and she knows she is loved. From time to time my grandmother's mother visits them from Osaka, where she has returned after years in the countryside, her brother's family having taken her in, and the road up the mountain is paved now, and she hires a car for the trip, the engine audible for miles, chugging up the road, until she crests the last hill before my grandparents' house like a vision of a better future, perched in the back seat, waving a white-gloved hand out an open window.

The world changes, and little by little the memory of the god-dess that my grandmother watched from the outhouse fades in her mind, until she begins to wonder if she dreamed it, if it was a fantasy of her years of grief. The boulder where Izanagi is said to have emerged from the land of the dead is different now, it looks smaller than it once did, and there is a parking lot in the adjacent field and a small sign put up by the neighborhood council and a clearing where teenagers drink and set off fireworks in the summer, and what power this land ever had for magic seems to dim. But the memory never fades completely, and on some nights when the old fear and suffering feel especially close, when hail ruins the persimmon crop or storms flood the fields in the valley or my mother's old sicknesses return, her fevers that last for days and weeks, how she shivers through the night, unable to sleep, my grandmother thinks of the goddess again, she remembers the light shining from the road, and she feels the old calm, the way it once unruffled her breath. And she sits by my mother's bed in the dark of the house, swallowing the familiar acid in her stomach, feeling it swell in her blood, and she tells my mother a story—a new story, one she has never heard, but that somehow, she thinks, feels right.

It goes like this:

Izanami is a goddess who is drawn, in the end, to the living. Izanagi, her husband, tries to trap her among the dead by dragging a boulder across the threshold to the land of the living, but the boulder is not so big as he thinks, not to a god at least, and Izanami could move it, but she doesn't. For a long time she tends only to the dead, to the peasants and nobles that stream into her kingdom, and then the soldiers and civilians, the broken bodies of panicked boys and wide-eyed girls, and centuries pass like this, how she tries to heal the wreckage of things, until one day she passes by the entrance of the tunnel that leads out of the land of the dead, and stops. Even gods and goddesses need time to heal, and at first, after a pause, she walks away from the entrance, and this happens again and again over the years, because she is afraid of the land of the living, of what she might find. But at night she will be drawn back to the entrance to the tunnel, and she will feel an itch growing in her blood, and she will not know if she's ready, until finally one night she walks into the tunnel, and makes the long journey to the place where it dead-ends at the boulder, and she thinks of moving it but decides, in the end—because she isn't showy like her husband, because this is a private magic—to dig a small hole to the side of the boulder, somewhere off in the forest, where no one will see it, and steps lightly into our world.

At first the goddess isn't sure what she is here to do, because pain is a sort of smoke, it covers up the past, but she knows that something calls to her, and she follows that call through the forest, down mountain roads to a small town and then a valley and all the way to the city, until she glimpses the sea, and she knows.

It takes her more than one try. Even for a goddess, it isn't easy. She goes back to her kingdom, and returns the next night, feeling stronger, and each time she makes it farther and farther. When at last she is standing at the water, when she is at the edge of the ocean, she bends down until her lips touch the water, and she finds her children there, as she knew she would, her very first children who neither lived nor died but collapsed like bubbles into water and made their way over centuries through creeks and rivers to the sea. The children are faint, they are scattered through the whole ocean, and it fixes nothing that she can find them here, after all these years, but still she bends to the water, and it both soothes her and breaks her, to feel her children so close, so that after she does this, when she finally stands up again, she is not better, but changed. And later, when she returns to the land of the dead, her life is mostly the same, except she finds she is able to cross more easily into the land of the living now, which she does from time to time, a sort of ritual that becomes comfortable with repetition, and she visits with her still-living kids, which she has not done for many years, and they greet her in their homes in the trees and sky, in the sun and moon, and they are glad to see her, if surprised and a little distant, and this makes her both happy and sad, because they remind her of her first children, the collapsed ones, but also they are, have always been, so much more than that.

What happens then? my mother asks, after a long pause.

We sleep now, my grandmother says.

And then, as the sky starts to brighten, as the birds begin to stir in the trees, they sleep.

Nishina Sekio Imprisoned in Dreams

For him, Hell is other people's dreams. This man who when he was alive could see none but his own. By day he is dead at the bottom of the sea. Slender worms with suits of glassy armor come to pick out his eyes, hunt for pieces of his toes in the sand. By night he wakes to dreams of people he doesn't know. Meadows in Paris. Cities in clouds. The dreams are beautiful, and the beauty hurts him, this bloodless torture, the lives he could have lived.

Above him there are forty meters of water. The sun at noon is a tentacled ball; storms are passing shadows. Nearby, the wreck of the USS *Mississinewa* is a familiar wall. There was a time when he gave his life and so many others to try to push the U.S. Navy out of sight. Nishina Sekio. Boy warrior. Inventor of the 人間魚雷 (human torpedo). Dead at twenty-one. Now he is rooted to the same sandy bottom as the ships he tried to fight, ordinary dreams candling his vision in the dark.

He dreams of a drain at the bottom of the ocean. He dreams of water swirling, swirling. He dreams of baseball, and summer crowds, and rivers. He dreams of fast cars and ocean roads. Once, he thinks he dreams of his father, his lecturing face, the way he would glance down at his notes, glasses slipping from his nose, but it's gone, swirling swirling, roaring out of sight.

3

Q: What do you feel when you make a bad choice?

A: I feel my heart coming out of my chest.

—Interview with Xavi Hernández, 2018

I can go weeks without thinking of whales /
and they never think of me

—Gretchen Marquette, *May Day*

My Father and Shigenobu Fusako in the Hallway of the Hotel New Otani, 1980

She was still a figure of romance then: Shigenobu Fusako, revolutionary leader, international fugitive, leaning against the yellow wallpaper of the Hotel New Otani, shoulder-length hair, polka-dot blouse, long fingers holding a cigarette. My mother says this couldn't have happened, that Fusako was in Beirut in those years by all accounts, dodging the CIA, commandeering the Japanese Red Army, but my father says he knew: those movie star cheekbones, the carelessly raised right hand, palm-up, pinching a cigarette between her thumb and forefinger, right elbow held close to her stomach, left arm hugging her waist. Years later, when they finally caught up to her in Takatsuki, an old woman disguised as a businessman living out of an extended-stay hotel, the news anchor said the cops had recognized her by the way she smoked, that same gesture, and my father leapt off the bed. My mother was in her pajamas on the floor in front of the TV, bath towel around her head, doing her evening stretching routine, egg timer going off every ninety seconds at her feet. She said my father was crazy, how could he possibly believe, after all these years, a wanted criminal in a hotel hallway, and doing what, just standing around, as if it didn't matter who saw her, but my father, making senseless gestures with his hands, still believed.

1980, a boom year. My parents flush with cash and possibility, not engaged but expecting it soon enough, taking their bright-red

Gemini down eight hours of highway to Tokyo and further to Izu, their first real adventure together, roughing it, car camping on the beach and in between, for a change of scene, fancy liqueurs, luxury hotels. This was the year a truck driver in Ginza found a hundred million yen wrapped in a handkerchief on the side of the road and got to keep it, months later, after he reported his find to the police and no one came forward to claim it. An effortless, impossible time: *Japan as Number One*, the book on everyone's mind, written by an American no less—today the number one auto manufacturer, tomorrow the number one economy, Japan on its way to the top of the world. The golden middle of an economic miracle, easy money for many, jobs for all, fortunes tossed aside on sidewalks, riches from rags.

My parents wanted to stay an extra night. A gray morning, light breeze, sky sealed off with clouds, and no schedule, no place they needed to be. The guestroom phone had entirely too many buttons to understand and my father, shoeless in checkerboard socks, headed into the hall. 独身貴族 (childless royalty) was what my mother said about those socks in those years, the way he spent money on little things without thinking, a conversational English teacher with no commitments or expenses and a drawerful of linen socks, silk, wool-blend on rainy days, shoeless on grass, on sand, as though money was a thing you could step in and throw away. My father had grown up a foster child in Boston in a home that treated him as undesirable, a recurring expense, and he insisted on this, that he was a man worth wasting on, that he had a right to be foolish in the smallest ways. My mother had grown up a farm girl in the middle of nowhere, a nowhere town in the mountains an hour's drive from Nowhere City, Japan, until she left for Osaka and a sales job and this: an undreamed-of future, pearled by rain, shimmering up at her through plate-glass windows from ten floors below.

The stranger noticed my father first in the hallway, as she would, a seasoned guerilla, twenty years on the run. Good evening, she said, in English, a clipped accent she must have picked up somewhere abroad, and my father, who had just the last week spent two hours filing and then unfiling residency papers across the counter from a wanted poster of her face (thick eyeliner, dark lipstick), height (155 cm), and birth date (September 28), found he had stopped walking: just like that, by the time he noticed, his legs were still. A Hollywood moment, blood rushing through his ears, anything could have happened, she could have had a gun, could have pulled a carbine out from behind her back and my father, willing himself calm, said: Hello. Beautiful weather.

It had drizzled all morning. The hallway was windowless. Maybe the stranger had seen the weather, maybe not. She nodded.

Well, my father said. He fumbled for words.

Do you smoke? She lifted her hand, a light movement, shoulders shifting, unclasping her left arm from her waist.

No, my father said.

This isn't your room, she said.

Right, of course.

And my father could move again, down the hall into the elevator and out to the ground floor lobby where he doubled back, realizing he had left the one woman he loved oblivious and alone in a room down the hall from a notorious taker of hostages, hijacker of planes, and steeled himself, for a long moment, in the elevator, before walking out. It had been a minute or two, at most, but the stranger was gone. My mother was taking a shower in their room. By the time she was done, my father had packed their things. They didn't call the police. Even then my mother doubted him immediately, talked him down from conviction to creeping anxiety, just enough fear to skibble down the hallway, just enough excitement to laugh about it in the parking lot, their bags slung over their shoulders, climbing into the car.

Take me away, my mother said. My father was driving. Once, he'd been a mechanic. Before that, he'd worked demolition and showered at the Y. Eight thousand miles westward, and that life was a fiction, a story that didn't matter if it was true or false.

Close call, my father said, starting up the car.

No chance, my mother said, pushing back her seat, kicking off her shoes. For so long, all through her childhood, she'd wanted this feeling: the road under her feet, leaving the world behind.

Late June, the Hotel New Otani, 1980. A year when the past seemed not to matter, when the future was an empty room. Here are my parents in their Gemini, pulling into the road, who know nothing of the lives that are waiting ahead of them. And here is Shigenobu Fusako, wherever she really is, in Beirut or in a room above them, at the peak of her illusion—of hope, of fearlessness, of change through violence, how she wrecked lives in the name of progress—holding a cigarette, repeating a gesture that in twenty years, another life, outside a different hotel, will return to her, and give her away.

Or Go Further Back

There was a time when my father lived on a boat, a twenty-five-foot sailboat he owned by himself in San Francisco or Oakland or somewhere and my mother was dating a man who owned a red convertible in Osaka, driving the coastal highway down to Kobe and Awaji and over the bridge to Tokushima and everywhere else. They went where they wanted and stayed as long as they needed and lived for only themselves. Later, on the night she married my father, my mother would take a last drive with this ex-boyfriend, his mortgage banking job, his ruby RX-7, radio dial phosphorescing in gold and teal and purple, and my father would wait at a friend's place, feet lofted on a table, drunk and worried and endlessly patient. Were they happy? They were who they chose to be. My father restored houses for a living and loved it and hated it, the chemical sting of the paint in his eyes and the wrestling with wood and mold, the feeling of rehabilitating something, what he could do with his hands. Once he'd been a foster child, nervous and silent in family court at ten years old. Once he'd slept in a van and worked demolition, showered at the Y every other day, and now this. My mother was working an anonymous office job and she loved it and hated it, the idea of it, how she had come out of the country, the deepest smallest country town, and now here she was in the dazzle of lights, her tiny apartment, her friends who only knew one part of her, the part that she wanted to become her, that she became. They were who they chose to be, my parents—nobody forced them to change or stay the same. My mother with her big-city accent and her foreign books and her stubbornly country tastes. How she could work magic in a garden. How she always chose fit over fashion. Her endless talent for language and her hands that could fold a whistle from a leaf or pull a cow to slaughter. Or go further back: once, my mother and father believed they could choose who to be, and for many years, a little while, they chose, and chose, and chose—

Elastico

I got a haircut today, and the whole time, in my mind, I was back in Kobe, Japan. My eyes closed, the bits of hair falling past, kissing my cheeks, the hair clipper motor whirring in my ear. The joke is that the place was called American Haircuts—this was in Oakland, near the Nimitz Freeway—and it faced a street named California Ave. The barber, who was from Taiwan, kept telling me my hair was a stylist's dream. He thought I should be a hair model, he said, which was probably just flattery, but still, when I got home, I looked it up. I thought the job would be kind of like a hand model—the photographer's lens carefully cropping out one body part, my scalp the *after* in the Rogaine ads—but it turned out what he meant was a person who sits on stage and lets high-end barbers strut their stuff at international conventions. It turns out everybody, even barbers, have to go to conventions.

There aren't a lot of buzz cuts in Japan. At least there weren't when I lived there. Even the subway station near the house where I grew up, which for a while offered ten-dollar haircuts from cosmetology students just outside the turnstiles, used only scissors. I did get my head shaved once though, at the end of high school, a few months before I left the country. My parents didn't know about it, and I spent the whole train ride home coming up with what I wanted to tell them. I got further than I expected with my mother, who raised a hand to her mouth when I told her there'd been a fire at school. But my father, at the door, just laughed.

You can see me in the graduation pictures. Some people go bald and they look younger, or kinder, or they look like a monk. I looked like a neo-Nazi. At least that's what my father said, shaking his head.

That was the year I played on the soccer team. It was just after the World Cup in France, and we all wanted to be Ronaldo or Zidane. The Japanese team had still not won a single game then, and we only knew a handful of the players well. We were all practicing roulettes on the pitch before practice, or on the sidewalk on our way to the station, and our coach had to tell us before the last game not to play at a higher level than what we were.

Basir, the keeper, was the one who'd held the clippers. Maybe it was the coldness of his hands, the spread of them across newly exposed skin, like that trick we used to do where you brush outward on a friend's kneecap with your fingertips so it feels like breaking an egg, that made me remember. Isn't it funny how with some things, not thinking about it is like locking it away? Years later, lifting open the lid, you hold it up without even a speck of dust.

Those were the days when I looked different but felt the same. It's odd how now in America I look the same but feel different. I went to dinner at a friend's place a few weeks ago, and there was a quiz before dessert to decide who was the most Japanese. It was for fun, and we laughed, and anyway the questions were full of errors, but at the same time, it was goddamned serious. Our laughter got quieter over time.

It was important in high school too, being Japanese, but the answers seemed more clear-cut then. If you could be articulate, and you didn't have an accent, you were in. At least that's how I thought of it. The trajectory of my life was that I grew to look more and more like my father with age. In twelfth grade I was just at that point where the checkout clerk at the grocery store would sometimes complement me on my Japanese. I would say: Would you believe it? I was born in Kyoto, and we would laugh, and that was still enough for me then.

The school I was at taught most of its classes in English. This was the one that was mostly for mixed kids and the children of immigrants, whose parents were either hoping to move back at any moment or had, like my father, panicked when they realized that for years we had been answering in Japanese to questions they posed in whatever language.

If foreign-language instruction was what you wanted, there weren't a lot of options, and this was one of those small schools that stays afloat by charging as much money as it thinks you can stand. It was built next to a container terminal on a piece of land that had folded like a card table in the last big earthquake, but still, the cost was everything we had. Of course, there were only so many things my parents could manage not to say aloud. I remember long, grueling fights between them, and afterward my father in my room alone, or in the shed behind the house, making it clear to me that my future was the thing that was driving them under.

I watched the World Cup religiously. It was hard not to see. '98 was the first time Japan had qualified at all, after the disaster in '94 that people called the Tragedy of Doha. In the spring the buildup to the tournament was all over the news, and everyone, from the department store in town to the candy store in the arcade down the street, was dusting off a television or, failing that, a radio, and setting it up in the storefront or behind the counter. All the talk was about whether Japan could make it in the world until one of the players, in an interview, asked if we'd ever been out.

The 7-Eleven held a lottery through the spring and summer where all the prizes had to do with soccer. I got the fifth-place prize, a tournament ball painted green and orange, and like a true prodigy I walked the neighborhood for months with it glued to my foot. I liked the abandoned lot up the hill because it had a half-sunken parking space, and on the low cinderblock wall I scratched two lines with a rock eight yards apart.

Not bad, the coach said one day at school. The soccer coach was also our gym teacher, and every year he taught a month of five-a-side, where anyone on the team was allowed to get lost. Fooling around in the corner, I'd just pulled off one of the only rainbow kicks I would ever get right. The ball landed sweetly in my stride, but when I heard the coach's voice I got nervous, and bent down to pick it up. When class ended he pulled me aside and said, got any cleats?

God, if I had made it as a player, what a story this could have been.

Hideto, the captain, was the one who really held the team together. The coach only decided who was in and who was out. But it was Hideto who decided that we would show up for practice at seven in the morning and keep at it until school began, and again from the end of the last class to whenever it got so dark that the ball was a flash of silver in the distance, taking shape on approach. Our coach had a kid he had to pick up from preschool at four-thirty, and that meant most of the time he wasn't even around.

It was grueling and it was freezing but it was beautiful too, though beauty is the kind of thing that's bigger in the rearview than when you're staring straight at it. From the pitch, looking through the chain-link fence, you could see the tops of the shipping cranes rising up from the harbor on the far side of a low berm of yellowed grass. The cranes were painted white with four legs and a long, straight neck, and there was always a moment at dawn or dusk when they seemed to disappear into the sky. When the boats arrived, the big Maersk ships with their multicolored containers and their size like whole islands, merging with the city, we would see the necks of the cranes dip downward, as if to take a drink.

It was a place that was famous for its ship-killing winds coming down off the mountains, though all we knew for sure was the way the cold could reach through layers of cotton as easy as winter travels through the nails in a wall. We were out there in long sleeves during practice, but on match days we couldn't wear anything that stuck out beyond our uniforms. Instead we walked onto the field with three t-shirts and two pairs of shorts underneath, looking like the Michelin Man at the beach with our matchstick arms and legs held out stiffly from barrel chests and heavy thighs.

Taking the train home together, the air filling with the smell of dirty socks and cheap deodorant, we lounged like kings. We talked or didn't talk, it didn't matter, and we were tired enough that laughter came easily. We spoke in Japanese, of course, unless there was something we wanted to keep private among ourselves. This might be about someone at school we didn't like, or about the man with the briefcase who always fell asleep on the train with a column of spit reaching down from his lips to his knee. We would start out with eight of us together—a few took the bus—and gradually at each stop more people peeled off, until at Ashiya it was only me and Basir, and then at Amagasaki, me alone.

My father would sometimes meet me at the train station because this was who he was. He said he needed a break, or he wanted the night air, and he would wave at me when I was still coming down the steps. He wasn't much into sports, but he tried not to needle me about it. He said he could tell the stiffness of my muscles from the way I walked.

It's only now that I think I understand how we saw ourselves as standing on separate icebergs, reaching across to each other with our hands. My mother was reaching for my father, my father for me, and I was reaching for what I thought was Japan. In Boston, when he was thirteen, my father had stopped speaking to his mother in her native Italian. This is one of those things that children are forever too young to understand. Even adults sometimes don't see that to a person desperately holding on to who they used to be, language is like a guardrail at the edge of a cliff. With my father, the understanding only came years later, when one thing led to another—loneliness to tiredness, tiredness to depression, depression to something worse—and finally his mother could no longer hide what she was fighting so hard to stop herself from becoming.

I remember my father at the table, surrounded by the dark. This was the week when he was told for the sixth year running that he was in danger of losing his job. His boss was a smug man with a pinched nose who was forever toying with the idea that a younger, more handsome faculty would boost enrollment at the language school. I knew next to nothing about my father's job but I knew the exact day, each year, when this happened. My parents fought around their anxiety like climbers skirting a crevasse, their weariness ramping up and up until they clashed about anything at all: some money spent without need, some chore not done or done too late. My father was fifty-three and already had the one job he thought he could get. His coworkers were in their twenties and thirties and they thought of themselves as on a brief adventure, a few years in some foreign place and then back home to restart the lives that were waiting for them—a family business that would be passed on to the next generation, a career they could decide on once they managed to find themselves. My father with his meticulously bindered notes and the long silver hairs sticking out of his ears, knowing any complaint from a student could be the end of him. My mother could not see this as a life that could last and my father could see nothing else.

Coming out of my room, I found him alone. My mother had stormed out some time ago, and I had been working up the courage to open the door. I remember the sudden closeness between us, the two of us like friends. It must have been something about the way he grew up that meant he would always be the one to try to convince me, in these moments, that things would be fine. He faced me with his tight smile, his far away eyes, and I pulled out a chair across from him. He never seemed to remember, during these fights that often started before dusk, to turn on any lights except the one above his head.

She'll be back, he said, in English.

I know, I said, in Japanese.

I don't know why at that moment I reached out with one hand to his head and tangled my fingers through his hair. The strands were soft and dense, like the pelt of an animal, and they feathered out from between my knuckles and turned silver in the light of the lamp. In happier times, a month or so later, my mother would compare this hair to a field of grass. The kind that's well watered and freshly cut, she'd say, where you can see the stripes from when they ran the mowers in different directions. This was my mother at her softest, still warm from her bath, on a week when she had saved enough of her paycheck to add a little to the pot she was hoping would take her and a friend on a vacation some day. She would tussle my father's hair and say you could lose things in there, small things like a whistle or a set of keys, and not find it for years.

In the World Cup, in '98, Japan lost every match. There were two against sides we would later understand were impossible to beat, and the third, at the end of June, was against Jamaica. By this point, elimination from the group stage was already decided. In the second half, two-nil down, there was nothing on the line. Even the old man at the candy store, still watching, walked away from the screen.

Nobody knew it then, but on that screen, through gritted teeth, Nakayama Masashi was running on a broken foot. Even knowing it, if you watch the replays, you can barely tell. Afterward, joking about it to a reporter, he said kids, don't try this at home, but it was already too late. We had seen him fifteen minutes from full time, the ball coming off his bum leg, scoring the consolation goal. We knew what he had done, and we knew who we wanted to be.

Who we almost forgot, on our way back home, was the man who had partnered Nakayama up top for almost the whole forty minutes that he was injured. His name was Wagner Lopes, and he gave the ball to Nakayama for the goal. He was a good player, and the team needed him, but even we thought there was something indecent about relying on a player who had once been a citizen of somewhere else. No one had told us yet, though maybe, at that age, we wouldn't have cared, that when he took the train with his Brazilian-born, Japanese-looking wife, they got the same abuse our parents did.

We forgot Wagner Lopes, and we decided, somehow, that the pitch was where the prize you got for winning was to belong.

Show them what we got, Hideto would say before a match. This would be on a Sunday against a neighborhood school, no tournament or championship or trophy in store, nothing on the line. We had no cheering crowds, no bleachers, not even any grass. Our ground was gray dirt shot through with shards of white quartz that tore into your thighs when you hit the ground. We played in snow or rain or in puddles that threw up rooster tails of water behind every ball. But we were dreaming, dreaming, with every step we took.

I remember, on match days, being alone on the field. When you're on it a soccer pitch is bigger than you would ever believe, and at times the other players are a thousand miles away. This is the kind of thing you don't see when you watch a game on TV. The pounding of your head, the shifting of your lungs, the way the fifty yards between the center circle and the goal lines is like looking backward at the beach after drifting out to sea. How there is a shout, or a whistle, and you squint into the rain, and all of a sudden the game is about the distance between one step and the next. That the pitch is like an ocean liner but behind every goal scorer is a player who could have stopped it if he'd only had another yard. That the difference between a poser and the real thing is the length of one stride.

Our coach, watching from the sidelines, never knew. He wore a baseball cap backward and he was always coming up with ways to lean onto the pitch without actually stepping in it. Crouched on three limbs with his bony neck hanging over the touchline, he shouted useless instructions in his reedy voice. *Get* it, he would say. Or else: Put it in the *net*!

After each goal kick, a hand on my shoulder, nudging me forward. Hey, Hideto said. Don't listen to him. You got this.

They called us J-League Curry.

I am talking about the players on the other teams.

I don't mean all of them, but some of them, a few of them—enough to count. This was after a commercial that played some years back where a kid named Masao eats a spoonful of the stuff and turns into Ruy Ramos.

There was also Jay Kabira, the pundit. Sergio Echigo, the retired player.

These were posers who were a step behind the real Japanese. This is what we thought back then. What I mean is that you wouldn't know from looking at them unless you knew what to look for, or else from listening to them if you didn't hear the jokes. For example, for a while there were people who got a lot of laughs out of quoting parts of Sergio's commentary where it sounded like he was saying something other than what he meant.

One of the ways the players made the comparison was to ask if we could do the elastico, like Sergio could. This was after a match, off the pitch, picking up our stuff from where we'd left it by the fence. A player from the other team came by, a younger player, the team clown, and he wanted to see an elastico. He wasn't able to do it himself, though in a few of the teams, some of the older players could pull it off easy. But a young kid was the one to ask, heels scuffing dirt, goofing off.

The elastico is one of those sleight-of-hand tricks that looks impossible until it's explained to you, and then you think, mistakenly, that it's easy. You push the ball one way with the outside of your foot, like you're planning to pivot to your right, and then somehow, without losing contact of the ball, you swivel your foot around so that now you're pushing with the inside, going the other direction. On a high school soccer team, when it's done to you for the first time, it hurts your mind to see it. You're convinced the guy is sprinting one way, until the split second it becomes clear, too late, that you've lost him.

I could do a rabona. I could do step-overs. I could even, given enough chances in training, pull off a couple of bicycle kicks. But I could never do the damned elastico.

Come on, the kid said, dribbling a ball toward me, feinting left and right. I want to see you try, he said. And then he pulled out a few crumpled bills he must have had in his pockets for exactly this reason, and said, what if I gave you money? How about then?

Fuck off, Basir said, sitting with his shoes off, airing out his socks. Who the hell cares how much money you got?

Look, Yūji said, getting to his feet. Yūji was one of the few guys on the team who was unimpeachably Japanese, and I think he knew, in times like this, that it was a question of taking a side. He said, your friends are over there kid, go bother them.

You want to join us, Masao? the kid said, finding the easy joke. He wasn't witty so much as he had a nose for the kind of territory where even the obvious lines hit hard.

All right, I said, all right I will, and I took the ball and the money from the surprised kid. Then I set the ball on the ground, and with less power than I would have liked, I booted it across the pitch.

So long, we said, every one of us pointing, or laughing, or waving him away.

We believed in the team. We believed in the game. We were convinced of our power to look after ourselves.

At home, later on, woken up by a pebble on the glass, I snuck downstairs and unlocked the door. My mother in the night, her hair over her face, still in the worn sweater she had on when she stormed out the door. Shivering in the wind, stomping her feet, she said *teamwork*, like that was all that mattered, and smiled her smile that lit up the dark.

Let me say one last thing about the World Cup.

This is the part people don't remember. The thing you won't hear in all the retrospectives or the nostalgic documentaries. Even I didn't know it then, though it seems important, now, to say it.

At the end of the tournament, when the team came home, one player wasn't even on the plane. He didn't meet the throngs of fans who mobbed the arrivals gate, he didn't pose for pictures by the podium, he didn't duck when someone threw a water bottle at Jō Shōji, the first-choice striker who'd missed every shot.

I am talking about the power of the game.

It goes all the way back to November, during the World Cup qualifiers, a few days before a match against Iran, when Wagner Lopes learned his mother had died of cancer. He was offered the chance to go home for her funeral, and he chose, instead, to stay. This was back when it looked as though the team wouldn't make it to the World Cup at all. This was when it seemed like Wagner Lopes, even if he stayed, might have spent the whole ninety minutes on the bench.

He chose to stay.

He must have thought, like we did, *I got this*. He must have convinced himself, against all reason, that he could make a difference. And when the match arrived, and he did in fact play, and he helped get the goal that meant they would go to the World Cup, one of his teammates, like an idiot, put an arm around Lopes and said, it's all thanks to your mother.

I am talking about the power of the game to turn us into idiots, one and all.

After the match the newspaper headlines read "The Triumph of Johor Bahru," naming the city in Malaysia where the qualifiers were held.

After the World Cup, the players coming home, the headlines read "Japan Wins Hearts, If Not Games."

Maybe Lopes didn't read them. He wasn't there. He was on a plane, at long last, to Brazil.

Our last match came in March after a long period of wintry weather. It was one of those times when, some mornings, we would find the buds on the cherry trees encased in ice. At first, during practice, the pitch was soft enough to sink into, but over the course of a week it hardened into a brittle crust that lifted up in sheets under our boots when we ran.

Basir, who'd had a great season, spun in circles at the end of our last practice: Behold, he said, I am the Asian Zidane!

A moment later, arms flailing, stumbling into a sprint: And now, he said, the Japanese Ronaldo!

Our coach, climbing into his van, rolling down the window: No fancy feet! he said. No tricky thinking! Tomorrow I want you to play exactly at the level you are.

When he left, we looked to Hideto, who'd taken an awkward knock a few days ago and was now all the more visible thanks to the tube net bandage that hovered like an enormous soccer ball around his head.

I'll be damned, he said, looking truly surprised. That's not bad advice, he said.

Crestfallen, we ran out the rest of practice with easy passing drills and jogging a few laps around the pitch. In the locker room, packing up, Yūji got a lot of mileage out of saying, for everything he did, that this was the second-to-last time.

This is the second-to-last time I'm ever going to pull off my cleats, he said.

This is the second-to-last time I'm ever going to take the lock off my locker.

This is the second-to-last time I'm ever going to smell these socks. And then he held them up, the socks, and we laughed and choked and pinched our noses and grabbed our things and fled the room.

My father, making an effort, said go get 'em, Champ. This was on a Friday, the match for once on a weekday, as I headed out the door. My mother, packing her things for work, grabbed me as I put on my jacket. She'd run track in high school, growing up in a small town in Hiroshima, and she knew exactly what to say. Be smart, she said, squeezing my elbow so I'd look her in the eye.

Fourth period, the sky swept clean, we stepped onto the pitch. Hideto, with his bandage like a crown, had us all circle up at the edge of our box. Our arms around each other's shoulders, we put one foot forward, like they do in the movies.

Show them what we got, Hideto said for the last time.

There were maybe twenty kids, let out of class, who watched us start. They sat on the dirt, or leaned against the fence, or some of them climbed the berm. Behind them, with the harbor in its off-hours, even the cranes held their heads up high as if to see what we would do.

Our last kickoff whistle. Our last nervous first pass.

Our coach, true to form, yelled Pass better! Keep the ball!

Hideto, true to form, picked up the pass, weighed his options, steadied the team.

On your right, we said, running forward. Man on, we said, turning back. You got me if you need me, we said, feet wide apart, facing the player with the ball, meaning that if he got too much in the thick of things, if he ran into a dead end, he could always pass the ball back, to us.

Push up, someone said, and we did. Get back, someone said, and we did. We did the little things, too, playing within our limits, doing the easy things right. I got this, we said, when we thought we could cut out a cross. Yours, we said, when we couldn't.

Get that guy, someone said. Hideto with the ball in the middle of the pitch, casting around, weighing his options.

Nil-nil. One-nil. One-one. There was a rhythm to the game that felt like breathing. Pressing forward and tracking back. Switching up play. Running into space. Touch, touch, pass. Touch, touch, shoot. We were a machine with eleven parts. We danced across the pitch.

First half, second half, extra time.

Our opposition was also well-drilled. They worked in lines. They hunted in packs. They passed with long balls from one side to the next. They doubled up on some players, they ignored some others. When Yūji got too fancy on the left wing, fumbling his pass, and Hideto had to sprint to get it, there were two of their players by his side. When I couldn't make it past my defender on the right wing, turning a step too late, and Hideto had to come out to win it back, there were two players converging on him even as I, without a marker, ran alone. They ran in a line of three, each one keeping pace with the others, trying to get in front. One of the players, a tall defender with a wide chest, held his shoulder in front of Hideto. The other player, a short midfielder with squat thighs and long arms, ran with his toes nearly brushing Hideto's heels. It was a normal play. There was nothing in it. The tall defender leaned into Hideto, keeping close, making sure of his place, and Hideto pushed back, trying to break through, putting up a fight. And when, in a jolt that could have been caused by anything at all, Hideto went down—one elbow clattering into the defender's back, both legs sliding into the midfielder's stride—I saw the midfielder cringe. The last play of the match, a white head sinking like a balloon behind the defender's shoulder, pressing into the dirt, and the midfielder above him suddenly unsure of his footing, his right shoe sinking into surgical fabric, slipping on gauze and then catching on something—a mesh, some bone—his face pulling tight, not in anger, but surprise.

In my mind, you understand, in my memory, I had time to think. We wore eight-pointed cleats, I thought, that rocked from front to back when you walked on pavement. We changed them once a season to keep the studs from wearing down. You might as well run someone over in skates, I thought. I should have turned one step before, I thought.

I should have been the real thing, I thought.

In the dirt: the midfielder sprawled out, the defender looking back, Hideto with his bandage torn off, lying three feet from his head.

Our coach running across the pitch from a thousand miles away, stopping midway to blow the last end-of-match whistle.

He's fine, I thought, but then I couldn't tell. His eyes were open. He was watching the sky. I could see his chest rising and falling. I could see the dirt in his hair. I could see the light against his eyes.

I'm fine, Hideto said all of a sudden, sitting up.

You're kidding, the defender said.

There was a drop of blood, just a drop, welling out of his hairline and pearling down Hideto's neck. The coach kept laying his palm to Hideto's head, as if he too couldn't believe.

I raised my hands to my face and saw that they were trembling.

We packed our things.

It wasn't much, though for some it was more than we thought. Yūji found a pair of glasses at the bottom of his locker he thought he'd lost. Basir found a sour-smelling towel. We put our cleats into shopping bags and tied the handles tight. We walked into the shower with our uniforms, to wash them off.

We weren't in the mood for shaving our heads but Basir had brought the clippers all the way from his house. We called it the Last Year Shear, and as far as we knew it had always been done. There was an old pipe stool in the coach's office, and a stack of newspapers in a closet. We set the stool atop Wagner Lopes, the World Cup—the whole year's events.

We went in turn: the six of us who were graduating. The last ones to go were Basir, who got me, and I got Hideto. We had our fun, of course, the mood lifting little by little, each of us, at some point, giving each other what we thought of as the Zidane. This was a perfectly circular bald spot the size of a soup bowl at the top of our heads. We loved everything about Zidane except his hair.

Look down, Basir told me, stepping back, turning off the shears. He'd shaved my hair in quadrants, and now he turned to the others.

The BMW, he said, deadpan, though most everyone was already laughing.

When I shaved Hideto, I didn't laugh at all. From up close I could see where the blood was from. Pressing his head to my chest so he wouldn't move, he smelled like iodine and dandruff and salt. You always wonder if there will be something unexpected on someone's scalp, like odd bumps or dark spots, but all I could see were faded scars and a field of red dots where the bandage had been. I held my breath when I ran the clippers on either side of the cut, skirting around the bright blue sutures that must have come loose in his fall. There were drops of dried disinfectant on the side of his head, like a spray of oat-colored freckles tumbling down to his ears. When I finished shaving there were streaks across my shirt.

It felt like the end of everything, and the end of nothing. It was hard to believe, back then, that things could change. We thought we would always be a team. We thought we would be there for each other. We thought we could count on the places we knew. We had no idea of our normal, quiet, tragic futures up ahead. How half of us would leave this place and never come back. How half of us would try to stay. How my father would be let go from the language school in a few short years, and how my mother would pack her things and leave for Hiroshima for eighteen months, gathering her thoughts. How Basir's father would drink so much convenience store liquor one night that he would reach for his sleeping pills and end up in the hospital. How Hideto would go to school abroad, then drop out, then head home, and how when they found him strung up against the door of his old room in his parents' house, the only numbers they would find in his phone except ours would be some taxi company in Florida. How our world, and the place we thought we had in it, was already breaking away, steaming down the channel, the tugboats like ants heading back to their nest, and us on the back deck, not even waving goodbye. How I would end up in American Haircuts, on California Ave, and the only home I know is in my head.

It's nothing special, I know. But I hold it up, after all this time, without a speck of dust.

There would be school again on Monday, we said, cleaning up a few last things that evening, long ago. There would be gym class, we said, for some of us, midweek. We told each other we had chores to do, schoolwork to catch up on, and without saying much else, we headed out into the hall.

Something feels off, Basir joked, clapping a hand to his head when we walked outside.

I'm a changed man, I said, and we laughed together.

It was the earliest we had taken the train home in months, and it took some getting used to. Nothing, it seemed, was quite the same. Not even the man with the briefcase, drooling on his knee, was there.

What My Mother Doesn't Say

プチ家出 *(petit estrangement)* though I wish she would, the French word making it silly, like a holiday, when she would storm out of the house, how we could have laughed about it together, after hours or days, my father at the table, me in my room, when she turned the car toward home, a woman resolved.

ご褒美貧乏 *(treat-yourself poverty)* though she must have wanted to, the fights she used to have over my father's spending, "If it weren't for money we'd have never fought," my father once told me when it was the two of us alone, although I'm not so sure.

心臓に毛が生えている *(there's hair growing on my heart)* to an old friend or confidante, how she learned not to take notice, how she must have held her tongue in waiting rooms when people asked whose child it was who had come in with her, who sat on the shrink-wrapped sofa waiting for her, who looked up with the hopefulness of a child toward a parent when she approached. One time, at a volunteer fireman's carnival in Virginia, a stranger learned my ethnicity and turned back to his friends to tell them about men traveling through Asia for sex, how they were sometimes trapped by children. He called this "yellow fever," and I wanted to punch him in the face.

イエローキャブ / 羅紗緬 / パンパンガール or any of the other names for women who start families with foreigners. She doesn't say the gazes of strangers carve her open. She doesn't say that gossip bitters her blood. My mother who makes her burdens look effortless, who teaches me grace.

どうにもなるよ *(it will all work out)* is what, once, she almost says. Instead she says ダメなもんはダメ *(if not, it won't)*.

The Failings of Our Fathers

When he mocks an American accent, the voice he uses is his father's. To-KY-o, he says, carefully placing the emphasis in the wrong place. Ki-YO-to. And then he laughs, and his friends do too. They laugh.

As long as he can remember he has wanted to be liked, and lately he thinks he may be having some success. His body has begun the process that comes to many mixed kids—the change from vagueness to definition, from genetic ambiguity to something crisper, confined. His hair has gone from vines to tussled. His neck from stalk to trunk. Last week, on the way from school to karaoke, a girl turned to him and asked, Do you sing?

Now he says ari-GA-to with that flagrant American *r*. He says dai-JOU-bu with that unnecessary *u*.

They are in a cheap place next to the monorail station. There is pleather on the chairs and old Asahi Beer posters on the walls. The girl who asked him if he could sing is slipping in her seat, leaning against his arm. Fourteen years old, and he believes he has never been this close to love.

He stays late. His father checks his watch as he stands outside a bank. They walk in together, and the bank clerk looks between them, and his eyes settle on the son. The father speaks English. The son translates.

His voice is flat, his thoughts are elsewhere: The click of the air conditioner coming on. The lazy spinning of the ceiling fans in her eyes.

Later his father takes him to an ice cream place, for thanks.

Incredible Lifelike Whale Comes Up for Air, Again and Again

My father's funeral: my aunt says a few words, my mother cries upstairs, and I sit in the boarding area of gate 23B, Guam International Airport, watching the silent news on CNN. Anderson Cooper tells me these are trying times for migrants and I tell him I know, I know.

Later, on the phone, my aunt asks me how I could have missed two different connections. First LA, she says, and now. Again. This is the same thing the Delta representative said. She said we kept trying to find you, where were you?

I tell my aunt my name was the problem. Twenty hours in flight and my head was nothing but ginger ale and airplane air. The thing about my name: with so many varieties, if I don't focus, I'll miss it.

For example, my first name. If the flight attendant is Japanese, my name is Gen, the way it should be. But in the hands of an American it will be Jen, or maybe Gene or Glenn or (sometimes), in a fit of bold invention that always amazes me, it will morph into Jennifer. This is why it's tough. Someone makes an announcement for Jennifer, and until some bleached-blond girl picks up her backpack and walks to the gate, I can't be sure it isn't me.

And then my last name. If I check in with my American passport, it is Del Raye. People always want to know if Del is a middle name. Sometimes the computer doesn't bother to ask, and the announcement ends up calling for Mr. Ray. On the other hand, if I check in with my Japanese passport, it is Hiroe. Outside of Japan this almost always turns into hero, as in the second part of superhero. No matter how often this happens, I can never learn to expect it.

I remember my father always used to enforce the right pronunciation. Maybe he spoiled me. When I was a kid and we traveled together, I could count on a pause and then the click of the intercom coming back online. Excuse me, it would say. That announcement was for Gen Del Raye, not Gene Ray. Mr. Del Raye, please come to the counter immediately.

The one time my father wasn't there, I remember, I was twelve and I was going to visit a friend who had relatives in Chicago. This was some years ago, when airlines had more money, and if you were a minor traveling alone on a route with layovers they would assign you a flight attendant to babysit you from the moment you got off one plane until you walked onto the next. Flying out of Osaka, they put out an in-flight announcement to tell me this. I was eating ice cream at the time (they had bumped me up to business class) and I was blissfully unaware until the moment I stepped through the gate and a woman in a red uniform picked me out of the line and said good afternoon, Mr. Hero.

I remember being confused and more than a little delighted. For a full two days, until my friend had to correct one of the neighborhood kids who came over to play, I kept wondering what I had done to make a pretty lady (and what twenty-something woman is not pretty from the perspective of a twelve-year-old?) call me a hero.

It ended like this.

Neighborhood kid: Hero? What kind of name is that?

My friend: Hiro-e, with an e.

Neighborhood kid: Hai-roi?

They called me Hey, Roy for the rest of the trip.

Maybe some part of me never got over trying to live up to that name. A sudden accident and the funeral home calls to say they want to do the funeral immediately. My mother wants to put it off, but I tell her it's okay. I can make it work. Take the flight from Boston to Houston and then Los Angeles. Overnight to Guam and then to Haneda and finally to Osaka. Somehow this shaved off four hours from the regular route and got me to the funeral with two hours to spare. This was, of course, before I missed my connections. The attendant at the gate gives me one piece of good news. I will still miss the funeral, but the next available flight, in four hours, goes direct.

My aunt is fond of saying that hero is only one letter away from zero.

Other times I tried to be a hero: I swam out to rescue my dog from a current in a river, and had to get rescued myself. I tried to resolve a fight between my parents about their finances by loaning them the contents of my piggy bank. Another time, on vacation in Okinawa, I took my father to the emergency room. I remember this was in a place called the Holiday In (the missing n was intentional), and while my mother tried to find someone to stop the air conditioner from leaking directly onto the bedspread, my father, in the dark room, wasting away with heat stroke, pulled himself up on his elbows and said son, this is your moment. I took my moment. An old van, driven by one of the motel proprietors, got us to the hospital eventually, and just that one time I really did save the day.

I remember waiting at the airport for the flight back, just a few gates away from this one, I picked out a toy whale that could really swim and my father paid for it. For your troubles, he said.

It turned out it was much easier to pretend. My last year in high school, I got elected class VP on the strength of my name alone. My campaign posters said "LET ME BE *YOUR* HIROE." People still remember that. My friend, who made up the other half of the ticket, went with something more staid, like "Yamada: Leadership you can trust." Nobody remembers that he won.

This is not just something that works in high school politics. It happens among adults too. I once saw a poster for senate reelection that said "Vote YES for Noh!" Sometimes I dream about calling that man up. It will be the middle of the night, late May, just before the filing deadline. He will reach for the phone in the darkness, and when he picks up, I will breathe into the receiver. Hello, I will say, this is your worst nightmare speaking.

My father would have wished that I had actually run. He wouldn't say it, but I knew. My father, who had wanted to be an astronaut, a zoologist, a professional sailor, and had to settle for teaching English as a second language in Japan. Every year the school would give him an allowance for classroom materials and he would use it up on a textbook on oceanography, or a dissecting microscope, or a boxed set of Jacques Cousteau DVDs. So of course when I have to split two thousand dollars across two VISA cards just to get home, I think of what my father would have said. He would have said look, I can't pretend I'm not in the same boat as you. But just . . .

He's right. Running for office, I would have been happier. I would have been one of those glad-handing politicians, promising to fix neighborhood potholes, put extra streetlamps on dangerous intersections. Behind the scenes I would have been cutthroat and ruthless. I would have employed a guy whose full-time job was to plant embarrassing and unsubstantiated rumors about the opposition. I would have been the second coming of Huey P. Long. I would have chartered a plane to bring my father's funeral to *me*.

I remember the year I got elected class VP my father went around telling everybody how I was devoted to politics, how he could see that I was made for it, even from an early age. He would say that after my parents refused to accept the contents of my piggy bank that one time, I made them promise to stop fighting in exchange for *not* taking the money, and when he finally wrapped his head around this reverse extortion, he knew. A joke, actually, but when I told him I was dropping out of college after the second year he really did ask: what about your dreams, your political future?

My mother would have said he loved you anyway, and with that *anyway* she would have been right. Living small in downtown

Hartford, doing the odd translation for cash and then blowing it all on travel abroad—he loved me anyway. He would have done almost anything, if I had needed it.

This is what I would have said at the funeral if I had made it on time.

Two hours before my new flight, and I go looking to see if they still sell that swimming whale. My mother would be glad to be reminded of it, and maybe afterward I could sneak it into the urn with his bones. I remember it was built like one of those old submarine toys. You'd put a spoonful of baking soda in its back, and when you'd set it down in your bath it would dive and come up for air, dive and come up for air again. This used to confuse the hell out of my dog, who would sniff at the spot where the whale went under and jump back in fright when it popped to the surface.

Sometimes the dog would bite at it, trying to snatch it in his mouth, but the way the toy was made, if you jostled the water more than a little bit, it would pop out a bubble from the compartment in its stomach and duck underwater, almost as if it knew.

The deal my father made was that if I could explain exactly how it worked, I could take an extra day off school. So that Monday, he called in and told the office I'd caught the stomach flu during my winter break. I remember him winking at me, his voice becoming subdued in the same way that my mother's voice went high whenever she spoke on the phone. He even made me talk a little, not to offer proof, but just for the amusement of acting, my father holding my nose so I would sound stopped up. When it seemed that we wouldn't be able to delay our laughter for another moment, he hung up.

We went into the city to watch a movie. I picked *Jurassic Park: Lost World*. My father was still a little tired out from the heat stroke a few days before, and not long after the lights went out he fell asleep. I had to go to the bathroom, so I snuck out to the hall.

I was walking back past the concessions stand when I heard some girls in line for popcorn say, in Japanese, I bet you could get *that* one. I turned to them just as they were looking away and giggling. There were four of them, all older than me, and they had come to the theater by themselves instead of with their father or mother. But still, I kept my cool. Only a few days ago I had saved my father's life. This is what I told myself. So I spoke up—try me—and one of the girls, instead of being embarrassed, said, I'm Shizue, who are you?

I said, I'm the boy that's going to ask you out.

Did I really say that? And *why* did I think it was a good line?

My aunt likes to say that every man is popular with the ladies at least three times in his life, and this was my first time. The girls were sneaking in to watch the second half of *Titanic*, and when they sat down in the last row I was in the seat next to Shizue. At night, out in the arctic sea in the lifeboats, when the theater went pitch-black, we held hands. Afterward, when we went to the arcade across the street, she looked pointedly at the others and we headed off, just the two of us, to the quiet corner with nothing else except claw machines. She picked out a stuffed dolphin, and for once in my life, though it cost me twenty minutes of mounting desperation and two fistfuls of hundred-yen coins, I actually managed to get it. It was dusty and unwieldy and faded on top like it had been sitting in that place for years. But when I handed it to her, and she smiled, the rush of tokens falling out of the change machine across the room echoed in my ears like applause.

She said, do you want to know a crazy thing?

She said, when dolphins dive their heart almost stops. Every time they take a breath, it's like coming back to life.

This was the moment: the two of us in the semi-darkness, Plexiglas all around us, a hundred lights moving and reflecting in our eyes. It was warm in the arcade but we were both wearing our winter coats. The way the light was, little slivers of color striped across our faces, I could see her heartbeat, could actually watch the shadow of it fluttering above her faux fur collar. It was strong and fast, the way I imagined it must be for a dolphin after a long time lost underwater, starving for oxygen, when it finally breaks the surface. I wanted to tell her this, but when I opened my mouth, nothing came out.

I was just thirteen, and she was a year older. I should have kissed her, but I didn't know.

She asked for my number. I didn't have a phone. She said that's okay. She said, if I give you my number, will you promise to call?

I said I promise. I said nothing will stop me. I said dependable is my middle name, and then I smiled to show that it was a joke but not a joke at all.

This is how the story ends: A dusty arcade, the music fading away and replaced by the crackle of the intercom. A high voice, probably a high school kid, speaking first too close and then too far from the mic. Delryu Gen, said the kid. Delryu Gen. And then the click of the mike turning off, and then back on, and my father's halting breaths.

Who knows how he found me. On the ride home I asked how he did it, and he said menacingly: you can't escape me that easy. But there must have been something about my face. Something that changed in my eyes that made him forget about all the time he must have spent on searching, all the fear he must have wasted. He said next time, come back before the movie ends, and I said yes sir, and that was that. He was that kind of father. And I was this kind of son: I never ended up calling Shizue. I didn't know what to say. I worried that over the phone, without any distractions, our words would run out. On weekends or after school, whenever I could get away, I would stand outside the movie theater, hoping to run into her.

I was the kind of kid who would rather wait for a miracle than risk seeing my luck run out.

Let's be honest. I'm still that kind of man. The quit-while-you're-ahead kind, or just quit-before-you-lose. The kind of person who, when I ran into my poli sci professor outside a laundromat three weeks after I left school, he said you had so much promise that first day you came in. The first *day*. Of course I dropped out. I didn't want to stick around for the fall, however slight.

Even now—feet propped on the cheap plastic seats, leaning around the CNN to see. From somewhere behind me, above but not too far away, the announcement goes out for the third time. It says final call for Flight 2173 to Osaka International Airport. Passenger Gene Ray, Gene Ray . . .

The intercom clicks off. Then it clicks back on.

It clicks off, and then it clicks back on.

Acknowledgments

I am indebted to everyone at the University of Nebraska Press and especially the following people for their help with the book:

Kwame Dawes, Cristina García, and Cate Kennedy, for believing in my writing.

Courtney Ochsner and Ann Baker, for their care in reading through the manuscript and for catching my errors.

Siwar Masannat and Abigail Kwambamba, for pulling everything together.

These people read and responded to early drafts of stories in this collection. I am eternally grateful for their generosity and insight:

Xue Feng, who has read my worst stories and somehow still sees the best in me.

Chavonn Williams Shen, who teaches me to think poetically and who writes all her comments in sparkly ink.

The Short Notice Readers, especially Rupa Thadhani and Meremu Chikwendu, who turn every Sunday and Tuesday evening into a soirée.

The Candid Agers—Michael Garberich, Megan 고은 Tulius, Anthony Shin, Bryan Wildes, Sarah 단비 Tulius, Wend C. Berner, Michael Montag, and Tim Dicks—for their remarkable voices.

And my teachers:

Carolina De Robertis, for embracing the literature of the margins and in whose class many of these stories began.

My dazzling MFA advisors Sheila O'Connor, in whose class I wrote my first ever "full-length" story, and John Brandon, who pushed me to see fiction in a different way.

Sun Yung Shin, for her skilled reading and encouraging words.

All my oceanography professors, who are still saving the world in ways large and small.

Stories in this collection previously appeared, in slightly different form, in the following journals: "Hideto, in Motion and at Rest" in *Passages North*; "My Mother Takes Me to a Public Bath" in *Storm Cellar Quarterly*; "Yukari Kneeling in My Mother's Garden, 1994" in Gulf Coast; "Half-Blind" in *Monkeybicycle*; "Nishina Sekio in a Tunnel Alone" in *Cease, Cows*; "Preparations, 2015" in *Storyscape Journal*; "Home Burial" in *Water~Stone Review*; "Housefire" in *Gettysburg Review*; "Harvest Mouse" in *Wigleaf*; "A Shark Is an Animal That Blushes When You Touch Its Face" in *Pacifica Literary Review*; and "Incredible Lifelike Whale Comes Up for Air, Again and Again" in *Buffalo Almanack* and *The Forge Literary Magazine*. I thank the editors for their help and support.

Lastly, my deepest thanks to my parents, who are not the mother and father depicted in this collection. No story could do justice to their courage, patience, and kindness.

Selected Sources

I am grateful to the chroniclers, reporters, and researchers who made this book possible. Here is a small subset of the authors and works I relied on most heavily:

Shimoji Lawrence Yoshitaka's excellent 「混血」と「日本人」: ハーフ・ダブル・ミックスの社会史 ("Mixed blood" and "Japanese": A social history of half, double, and mixed-race communities) was an invaluable reference for thinking about the current and historical place of mixed-race children in Japanese society.

赤紙：男たちはこうして戦場へ送られた (Draft letters: How men were sent to the front) by Ozawa Masahito and the NHK Reporting Team informed my understanding of the draft-delivery process in Japan during World War II.

Descriptions of the Kaiten torpedo, the suicide weapon co-invented by Nishina Sekio, were informed by 回天特攻学徒隊：回天は優れた兵器ではなかった (Kaiten special-attack student corps: The Kaiten was not an effective weapon) by Takeda Gorō.

Details about the experience of living through the war as a civilian were drawn from many first-person accounts, including ones contained in these anthologies: 忘れないあのこと、戦争：残しておきたい私の戦争体験 (War, the things I won't forget: Wartime experiences I want to keep alive), edited by Katsumoto Saotome and the Wasurenai Anokoto Sensō Publishing Committee; and 昭和二十年夏、子どもたちが見た戦争 (Summer 1945: The war as seen by children) and 昭和二十年夏、女たちの戦争

(Summer 1945: The women's war), both edited by Kakehashi Kumiko. The schoolyard exercise described in "Suicide Drills, 1945" was based on an experience recounted in 戦争中の暮らしの記録 (A record of wartime life), edited by Kurashi no Techō Magazine. The story "We Are a Woman Bombed / A Picture of Grace" was inspired by an interview that aired on *Ogiue Chiki's Session-22* on TBS Radio on the occasion of President Barack Obama's visit to the Hiroshima Peace Memorial on May 27, 2016.

Finally, for descriptions of life in small-town Japan before and during the war, I relied on 母たちの語りつぎたきことども (Stories the mothers wish to pass along), edited by the Shimane Prefectural United Women's Association and NHK Matsue Broadcasting Station. I am told my grandmother was a member of the women's association and had a part in the making of the book.

IN THE RAZ/SHUMAKER PRAIRIE SCHOONER BOOK PRIZE IN FICTION SERIES

Last Call: Stories
By K. L. Cook

Carrying the Torch: Stories
By Brock Clarke

Nocturnal America
By John Keeble

The Alice Stories
By Jesse Lee Kercheval

Our Lady of the Artichokes and Other Portuguese-American Stories
By Katherine Vaz

Call Me Ahab: A Short Story Collection
By Anne Finger

Bliss, and Other Short Stories
By Ted Gilley

Destroy All Monsters, and Other Stories
By Greg Hrbek

Little Sinners, and Other Stories
By Karen Brown

Domesticated Wild Things, and Other Stories
By Xhenet Aliu

Now We Will Be Happy
By Amina Gautier

When Are You Coming Home? Stories
By Bryn Chancellor

One-Hundred-Knuckled Fist: Stories
By Dustin M. Hoffman

Black Jesus and Other Superheroes: Stories
By Venita Blackburn

Extinction Events: Stories
By Liz Breazeale

If the Body Allows It: Stories
By Megan Cummins

What Isn't Remembered: Stories
By Kristina Gorcheva-Newberry

Vanished: Stories
By Karin Lin-Greenberg

Boundless Deep, and Other Stories
By Gen Del Raye

Printed in the USA
CPSIA information can be obtained
at www.ICGtesting.com
LVHW091225151223
766489LV00004B/432

9 781496 237453